Daddy Was a Gunman

"I'm not leavin'."

"Then do something."

Clint sat there, slouched, seemingly relaxed, staring up at the younger man.

"Damn you!" Bravo shouted, and went for his gun. As he did so, Clint kicked the chair opposite him into Bravo, knocking him off balance. Clint came out of his chair, closed the distance between the two of them and snatched the gun from Bravo's hand. Then he pushed the young man, sending him spinning and sprawling into the center of the room.

Clint closed in on him again, got down on one knee and asked, "Tell me who put you up to this?"

"Whataya doin'?"

"Keeping you alive," Clint said, then pointed the young man's own gun at him, cocked the hammer and added, "Maybe."

Bravo stared down the barrel of his own gun and asked, "W-whataya wanna know?"

THE GUNSMITH

319

OUT OF THE PAST

J. R. ROBERTS

J

JOVE BOOKS, NEW YORK

THE BERKLEY PUBLISHING GROUP
Published by the Penguin Group
Penguin Group (USA) Inc.
375 Hudson Street, New York, New York 10014, USA
Penguin Group (Canada), 90 Eglinton Avenue East, Suite 700, Toronto, Ontario M4P 2Y3, Canada
(a division of Pearson Penguin Canada Inc.)
Penguin Books Ltd., 80 Strand, London WC2R 0RL, England
Penguin Group Ireland, 25 St. Stephen's Green, Dublin 2, Ireland (a division of Penguin Books Ltd.)
Penguin Group (Australia), 250 Camberwell Road, Camberwell, Victoria 3124, Australia
(a division of Pearson Australia Group Pty. Ltd.)
Penguin Books India Pvt. Ltd., 11 Community Centre, Panchsheel Park, New Delhi—110 017, India
Penguin Group (NZ), 67 Apollo Drive, Rosedale, North Shore 0632, New Zealand
(a division of Pearson New Zealand Ltd.)
Penguin Books (South Africa) (Pty.) Ltd., 24 Sturdee Avenue, Rosebank, Johannesburg 2196,
South Africa

Penguin Books Ltd., Registered Offices: 80 Strand, London WC2R 0RL, England

This is a work of fiction. Names, characters, places, and incidents either are the product of the author's imagination or are used fictitiously, and any resemblance to actual persons, living or dead, business establishments, events, or locales is entirely coincidental.

OUT OF THE PAST

A Jove Book / published by arrangement with the author

PRINTING HISTORY
Jove edition / July 2008

Copyright © 2008 by Robert J. Randisi.
Cover illustration by Sergio Giovine.

ISBN: 978-0-515-14483-3

JOVE®
Jove Books are published by The Berkley Publishing Group,
a division of Penguin Group (USA) Inc.,
375 Hudson Street, New York, New York 10014.
JOVE is a registered trademark of Penguin Group (USA) Inc.
The "J" design is a trademark belonging to Penguin Group (USA) Inc.

PRINTED IN THE UNITED STATES OF AMERICA

10 9 8 7 6 5 4 3 2 1

ONE

Clint Adams stared down at the cards in his hand. He had three aces, and it was the best hand he'd had in the three days since he'd arrived in St. Joe, Missouri, three days ago. That wasn't saying much for three days of poker. The only good thing was that he'd been playing pretty low stakes up to now.

Today's game was a little different. There was some new blood at the table, as several of the earlier players had moved on for various reasons. They'd either busted out or had finished their business in town. The new players who had taken their places had not been averse to higher stakes, so sitting with three aces in his hand and more money in the center of the table than at any time in the past three days was good news.

Especially since this was draw poker and he had his three aces before the draw.

Two players had dropped out and the two remaining players were new to the game.

The dealer's name was Victor Michaels. He had only arrived in town that morning, and within an hour of checking into his hotel, he'd headed over to the saloon, where he'd introduced himself and joined the game. But not once had he said what his business was.

The other player still in the game was a drummer named Elias Wells. His drummer's case was at his feet, which he claimed was filled with women's underwear from Paris, France. He was hoping to place some items with a shop that sold ladies intimates.

Wells had to draw first.

"Three cards," he said. He had called Clint's twenty-dollar bet with a pair. It was the largest bet that had been made at the table in three days, and it had knocked out the other two players, both citizens of the town.

"Two," Clint said.

Michaels dealt two cards to Clint, then looked at his own hand and said, "Dealer takes one."

Logic said he was trying to fill a straight or a flush, or had two pair. Anybody else and Clint might have suspected a bluff, but the man had not yet indicated he was that type of a player.

Of course, he could have just been waiting for a large pot.

"All right, Mr. Adams," Michaels said, "you're the opener. It's your bet."

Clint was seated so that he could see the door and the rest of the room. He noticed someone peering over the tops of the batwings, eyes scanning the room. From his vantage point—seeing only the top of the head, the eyes and the legs—he assumed it was a boy, maybe thirteen or fourteen years old. His mother had probably sent him to bring drunk Daddy home for supper.

"I'll open for fifty."

"Fifty?" Michaels repeated.

"Too steep?" Clint asked.

"Oh, no, no," Michaels said, "not at all—for me, anyway. Mr. Wells?"

"Is it my turn?" the drummer asked.

"No," Michaels said, "I was simply asking if you objected to the size of Mr. Adams's bet."

"Fifty dollars? No, no, it seems quite reasonable to me."

"Very well," Michaels said, "then the bet is fifty dollars to me."

He studied his cards for a few moments before acting.

"I'll call the fifty," Michaels said, "and raise a hundred—unless that is too steep?"

He looked at Elias Wells.

"Hmm, oh. Too steep? I'm afraid—yes, I'm afraid that is too much for me . . . with these cards anyway."

He dropped his hand facedown on the table, then sat back with his arms folded to watch along with the other sidelined players.

"A hundred to me, eh?" Clint asked.

"That's right, sir."

Clint had played for much higher stakes than these, so a hundred was not going to deter him.

"I call your hundred, Mr. Michaels," he said, "and raise a hundred."

While waiting for the dealer to make up his mind about folding, calling or raising, Clint looked over at the door again. The kid had stepped inside and was asking a man a question, while pointing back in the direction of the poker game. Probably wanted to know what was going on.

"Well," Michaels said, "I've gone too far now to give it up. I'll have to call you and raise another two hundred."

"You have a lot of confidence in one-call draw, Mr. Michaels."

"Please," the man said, "since I'm about to take a lot of your money, why don't you call me Victor?"

"All right, Victor," Clint said. "Why don't I just push the rest of my money into the middle of the table and we'll see just how good your four-card draw was?" Clint asked.

TWO

"I'm afraid you've got a little more there than I do, Clint . . ." Michaels said, looking down at the money in the middle of the table.

"Well, I can pull some of it back if it's too much," Clint offered.

"No, no," Michaels said, "I'll just have to go into my pocket, if that doesn't offend anyone else's table stakes sensibilities."

"I don't think anyone here is offended," Clint assured him.

"Okay," Michaels said, drawing his wallet from his inside jacket pocket, "that looks like . . . about four hundred and seventy-five dollars?"

"Exactly," Clint said, "you have a good eye."

Michaels put five one hundred dollar bills into the pot and withdrew twenty-five dollars change.

"Well," he said. Then, "I think four kings is pretty good for a one-card draw, don't you, Clint?" Victor Michaels asked.

"I think that was damn good, Victor," Clint said. The man nodded, smiled and reached for the pot. "It would've been even better," Clint went on, laying his cards on the table, "if I hadn't drawn a fourth ace."

Victor Michaels looked poleaxed. The color drained from his face and he sat back while Clint raked the pot in.

"Wow," Elias Wells said, shaking his head, "how often do you get to see two four-of-a-kinds in the same game— and in the same hand?"

"I never did see it," one of the other men said.

"It's very rare," Clint said, "So rare, in fact, that you didn't see it this time, either. Not fairly, anyway."

"What?" Wells asked.

"Well, I guess that cleans me out," Michaels said, starting to rise, but Clint clamped his hand on the man's wrist to stop him.

"Mr. Michaels didn't get that fourth king from the deck," Clint told Wells.

"Well, where . . . you mean, he's been cheatin'?" Wells asked.

He reached for the wrist Clint was holding, felt up and down the sleeve.

"He ain't got nothin' up his sleeve," Wells said.

"That's because he got it from his pocket when he withdrew his wallet and most of us were looking at the hundred dollar bills he laid on the table. Go on, check his pocket. I'm sure you'll find the card he replaced in there with the wallet."

"I don't have to stand here and—" Michaels started, but Clint cut him off.

"Yes," he said, "you do."

Elias Wells open Michaels's jacket, reached into the inner pocket and pulled out the man's wallet—and a five of clubs.

"Son of a bitch!" Wells said, throwing both items down on the table.

"All right, all right," Michaels said, "you caught me. I'll just take my wallet and—"

"Leave it," Clint said.

"What?"

"You can go, but leave the wallet. These men lost money to you. They're going to get it back."

"But . . . there's two thousand dollars in there!" the man cried.

"That'll more than cover their losses," Clint said, "and buy a round of drinks for the house."

Their conversation had drawn some attention from nearby tables, and while not a lot of people knew what was going on, the news of a round of drinks spread like wildfire.

"That's it, Mr. Michaels," Clint said. "You can go."

"But I—"

"Get out while you can still walk," Clint said.

While Victor Michaels staggered out the door, Clint picked up his winnings and said to the rest of the men at the table, "Split that money up and leave enough for drinks for the house."

"That sounds good to me," Wells said.

"And just take what you started with," Clint added. "Don't be looking to make a profit."

"That's fair," Well said.

He and the other men opened the wallet and took what was theirs and then Wells shouted, "Drinks on the house!"

That wasn't exactly true, but it was close enough for everyone.

Clint walked to the bar and secured a place for himself, then signaled the waiter for a beer.

"Mr. Adams?"

He turned, then looked down to see the young lad who had been at the door looking up at him.

"Yes? What can I do for you?"

"Well, sir, you are Clint Adams, right?"

"That's right."

"I need to talk to you, sir."

"What about? You know, you shouldn't be in here. What are you, thirteen?"

"I'm almost sixteen."

"Sixteen?" Clint said. "You're a little small for your age, aren't you, son?"

"You might be right about that," the youngster said, "if I were a boy."

"What? You mean—"

"Yes, sir," she said. "I'm a girl."

"Well . . . then you really shouldn't be in here, should you? What's your name?"

"Sandy."

"Well, Sandy," Clint said, "don't you think your mother might be looking for you?"

"I don't think so."

"Why not?"

"She's dead."

"Oh, I'm sorry," Clint said. "Well, your father, then. Surely he's wondering where you are."

"I hope not, sir," she said.

"Why's that?"

"Well," she said, "I'm hoping I'm lookin' at my father right now."

THREE

Clint wasn't sure he'd heard right above the din of the men bellying up to the bar for their free drinks.

"Come outside," he said. He almost took the girl's arm, but then pulled his hand away as if she were hot.

Together they left the saloon and stopped outside on the walk.

"What did you say?"

"I said I think you're my daddy."

"What makes you think that . . . Sandy?"

"Well, sir," she said. "Momma told me."

"When?"

"Just before she died," Sandy said. "She told me to go looking for you if I ever needed help, because you'd help me."

He studied the girl standing in front of him. Her hair was chopped short but it was red. Beneath the grime she looked pretty—freckled face and green eyes. She stood about five foot two and she stared at him boldly, but he could see a hint of fear lurking behind those emerald eyes. Fear of him? Or that he might reject her?

"Who was your momma, Sandy?"

"Anne Archer."

Clint felt as if he'd been punched in the gut and stabbed in the heart at the same time.

"You knew my ma," Sandy said.

"Oh, yes," Clint said. "I knew her."

"Did you love her?"

Clint thought about the question. Anne Archer was a beautiful woman who also happened to be a bounty hunter. She had two partners, Sandy Spillane and Katy Little-feather. They were all exceptional women and very good at what they did, but it was Anne Archer he really connected with. Over the years their paths crossed and at times it seemed that they wouldn't uncross, but in the end they'd end up going their separate ways. It had been many years since he'd seen her, or even heard from her . . . and now this. He felt an ache that came not only from sadness, but from shame.

And now this . . .

"Are you hungry?" he asked. "I'm hungry."

"Yes, sir."

"Come on," he said. "We'll get something to eat and talk about . . . your mother."

He took her to a small café off the main street and ordered them two steak suppers. The kid ate as if she hadn't eaten for weeks. Clint ate his own steak, watching her the whole time. He thought he saw little flashes of Anne Archer, but what he was looking for was something of himself.

"You never answered my question," she pointed out around a mouthful of steak and potatoes.

"What question was that?"

"Did you love my mother?"

"Yes, I did."

"Why didn't you ever marry her?"

"I'm not the type to get married," he said.

"Because of your reputation?"

"And my nature."

"I don't know what you mean."

"It's my nature to travel. My . . . inclination. I can't stay in one place for too long. I get . . . itchy."

"I'm like that," Sandy said. "I want to travel. My mother says—said—I got it from you. I mean, from my father. That was before she told me who you were."

"When did your mother die?"

"A week ago."

That surprised him.

"Where?"

"In Kansas City."

"How?"

"Somebody killed her."

"Who?"

"I don't know," she said. "Nobody does."

"I don't understand. Was she working?"

"She didn't do that anymore," she said. "She was murdered."

"How did you know where I was?" Clint asked. "Who sent you to me?"

"My aunts."

"Aunts?"

"My mother's partners," she said. "Sandy and Katy."

"Sandy . . ."

"My full name is Sandy Littlefeather Archer," she said.

"Where are your aunts now?"

"In Kansas City," she said. "We heard that you were here. I took a horse and rode here."

"You stole a horse?"

"Borrowed," she said. "I'll bring it back."

"We'll bring it back," he said.

"You mean?"

"Eat up," Clint said. "We're going to Kansas City."

FOUR

Clint got Sandy a room at his hotel and told her to get some sleep, they'd be leaving early the next day.

In his own room sleep eluded him. Once before a young boy had claimed to be his son, and that had turned out to be a hoax. How was this one going to turn out? Back then he'd had a bit of a hard time remembering the woman the boy said was his mother, but this was different. Anne Archer was a woman who, under different circumstances, he might have married and settled down with, but neither of them were bred for that. They spent more time on horses than in hotel beds and wore a gun wherever they went.

He was pleased that both Sandy and Katy Littlefeather would be in Kansas City. At least he could talk to them about this. God, he hadn't seen any of them in . . . nine or ten years.

Wait a minute. Nine or ten years? And Sandy said she was almost sixteen?

He put his boots and trousers back on and went down the hall to her room. She answered his first knock, stared at him expectantly.

"Sorry to wake you," he said.

"That's all right," she said. "I wasn't asleep. Come in."

"That's okay," he said. "I have one question and I can ask it out here."

She had washed her face and he could see now that she was very pretty. He wondered if she kept her hair short and wore boy's clothes all the time.

"You told me that you're fifteen?"

"Almost sixteen," she corrected.

"But . . . I saw your mother and your . . . your aunts about nine or ten years ago."

"I was wonderin' when you'd get to that," she said. "I would've been around six. My mother said she didn't want to tell you about me back then."

"Why not?"

She shrugged.

"Only she knows why she kept me from you," Sandy said. "Or maybe you could ask Aunt Sandy."

"I guess I'll have to," he said. "Okay, you can go back to sleep . . . or to whatever you were doing."

"Can't sleep," she said. "Can you come in and talk a while?"

He looked up and down the hall, didn't see anyone, then said, "Sure," and stepped into the room.

Outside the hotel two men stood in the doorway of a building across the street.

"You think that was him?" one of them asked.

"Of course that was him," the other man said. "He got the girl a room, didn't he?"

The other man grinned and said, "Unless he put 'er in his room. Maybe he likes 'em young."

"You're a pig," the first man said. "She's supposed to be his daughter."

"Yeah, but maybe he ain't so sure," the second man said. "I mean, I seen that girl in a dress. She's kinda tasty."

"You're the one that likes 'em young," the first man said, "and that's because you're a pig."

"And I suppose you like old women."

"You know what?" the first man said. "Just don't talk to me. We're here to watch."

"I thought we wuz here to kill the Gunsmith and make sure he don't get to Kansas City."

"Yeah, well," the man said, "that, too."

"What about the kid?"

"What about her?"

"We supposed ta kill her, too?"

"My orders is to make sure the Gunsmith don't get to Kansas City. That's it."

"Good," the second man said with a leer. "That means we don't hafta kill the tasty little girl."

The other man looked at him and said, "You're a pig."

FIVE

Clint woke the next morning actually looking forward to spending the day on the trail with Sandy. They had sat up in her room for hours with her asking him questions about her mother and Clint telling her stories about the two of them as well as her two aunts.

"They ever tell you stuff like this?" he'd asked her.

"They said I didn't need to hear these stories," she told him, "but they're wrong. I need to know everything I can about my mother."

Clint agreed. Sandy and Katy might be mad at him for telling her the stories, but he'd argue for the girl that she needed to hear it. She had to know who her mother was, especially now that she was dead.

As he left the room, a lump came to his throat. He remembered that this was all about Anne Archer being dead. He hoped that the modernized police department in Kansas City would have a lead on who her killer was, or might even have caught him by now.

He walked down the hall carrying his saddlebags and rifle and knocked on young Sandy's door. She answered right away and smiled at him. That was another thing he had discovered about her last night, that smile. It was definitely her mother's.

"Ready?"

"I'm ready."

"Let's go see what kind of horse you, uh, borrowed."

"They're comin' out," the first man said, nudging the second man awake.

"Jeez," the second man said, stretching, "why'd we both hafta stay out here all night?"

"What do you care?" the first one said. "You slept the whole time."

"Slept pretty good, too," the second man answered. "Dreamt about that sweet little gal."

Ed Presser turned and stared at his partner, Hal Chance.

"Do you say stuff like that just to annoy me?" Presser demanded.

"What, you'll kill a man but you won't fuck a fifteen-year-old girl?"

"Damnit, Hal—"

"Okay, okay, forget it," Chance said. "Look, they're headin' for the livery stable."

"Good," Presser said. "We've got to get to our horses and get ahead of them."

"Why don't we just trail 'em?" Chance asked.

"Because that's the Gunsmith, Hal," Presser said. "He'll spot us before we go a mile."

"He ain't seen us out here," Chance said.

"You don't think." Chance frowned. "Come on. Lucky we left our horses at the other livery."

"We got time for breakfast?" Chance asked as he hurried to keep up with his partner.

Clint inspected the horse Sandy had ridden in from Kansas City. It was a mare that was about ten years old, sturdily built but not something that would be able to keep up with Eclipse if they had to run.

"She'll do," he said. "It may take us all day to get there, but she'll make it."

"I like her," Sandy said, patting the horse's neck.

"Good," Clint said. "If you like her so much, you can saddle her."

When they walked their horses outside, Sandy's eyes widened.

"Wow! He's beautiful."

"Yeah, he is," Clint said. "This is Eclipse. He was a gift from a very famous man named P.T. Barnum."

"I heard of him," she said. "You know him?"

"Yes, I do," Clint said.

She approached Eclipse and reached out to pat his neck.

"Be careful," Clint warned. "He doesn't like strangers."

But Eclipse stood by very quietly as the girl stroked his neck.

"I guess he likes you," Clint said.

"Sure he does," she said, "don't you, big boy?"

Her hands were gentle and Eclipse actually closed his eyes while she stroked him.

"Okay," Clint said, "that's enough of that. You'll put him to sleep. Let's get mounted up."

"Can I ride him?" she asked.

"I can't let you do that."

"Why? He won't hurt me."

"No," Clint said, "but he might like you so much that he'll hurt me when I try to ride him again."

SIX

The girl rode well, sat the horse just like her mother did. Clint told her so.

"You think so?" she asked, obviously pleased. "Aunt Sandy and Aunt Katy always said Momma was the best rider of the three of them."

"What else did they have to say?" Clint asked.

"Well, Aunt Katy told me never to tell Aunt Sandy she said this, but she said my mom was also the brains of the three."

"I think she was the one with the most ideas," Clint said.

"And was she the best looking?" Sandy asked. "I mean, Aunt Katy is really pretty . . ."

As Clint remembered, all the women had something to recommend them, and he'd never tell Sandy that he'd been to bed with all three when he first met them. After that, though, it was only Anne he took to his bed when they all crossed trails.

They continued to talk about Sandy's mother while they rode, and from time to time Clint stopped to allow the girl's mare to take a breather. It was about thirty-five miles to Kansas City and Clint knew Eclipse could have covered that much ground in half a day, but he wasn't pushing.

He was enjoying the ride.

Presser and Chance positioned themselves about five miles farther on. They found a good vantage point for an ambush, a place where they could be on high ground and catch the Gunsmith in a cross fire.

"I hate ambushes," Presser said.

"Why? It's the easiest way to kill a man," Chance said. "I heard that Wild Bill Hickok shot most of the men he killed from ambush."

"That's just stupid," Presser said. "Where did you hear that?"

"I just heard it," Chance said. "Kinda ironic that he got shot in the back, huh?"

"Hal, I don't even know why I ride with you."

"Yeah, ya do," Chance said. "You'd be dead without me."

Chance left Presser and went to take up his own position on the other side of the road. Presser considered putting a bullet in the back of his partner's head, but the Gunsmith might have heard the shot.

He got comfortable on his stomach with his rifle next to him and waited.

Clint passed his canteen over to Sandy, who took a short drink and passed it back.

"What did your mother tell you about me?"

"Not much," Sandy said. "She didn't have time."

They hadn't talked about exactly how her mother had been killed. He didn't want to make her go through it again.

"You ain't asked me how she got killed, exactly," she said, as if she'd been reading his mind.

"I wasn't sure you want to talk about it."

"I can tell you she was shot from ambush," Sandy said. "I heard my aunts say that. She didn't die right away, though, which is why she was able to tell me about you—but only just."

"So you came to find me just to see if I was really your father?"

"You're my father," Sandy said. "My ma told me so. I didn't need to see you to find out."

"So you just wanted to meet me?"

"Well . . . yeah."

"But?"

She turned in the saddle and stared at him.

"Mostly," she said, "I want you to find whoever murdered my mom and kill them."

Normally, he would have tried to talk her out of that frame of mind. He would have told her that the law had to handle it and bring the killer to justice. But he didn't really feel that way, so why should she?

"You ain't gonna tell me I shouldn't feel that way, are you?"

"You're a little mind reader, aren't you?" he asked. "I was thinking about it, but no, I'm not going to tell you that."

"Good," she said, "'cause I ain't gonna change my mind about this. I want whoever killed my mom to die for it."

"How do your aunts feel?"

"The same, but they won't tell me that."

"Well, I *will* tell you that," Clint said. "I want the killer to die, and I'll do my best to make it happen. That's a promise."

SEVEN

Clint moved even before the sound of the first shot started echoing. His first instinct was to knock Sandy from her saddle, and then hit the dirt himself. Lead chewed up the ground around him, which confirmed his first thought, that he was the target. It also confirmed that they were in a cross fire.

"Find cover," he yelled to Sandy, waving. "Stay away from me."

The horses took off, which was good. They wouldn't be hit by any stray lead.

Clint pulled his gun and looked for cover. He spotted both men and knew instantly that they'd made a mistake in their choice of location. There was cover for him on the right side of the road in what looked like a small dry wash, and from that position the man firing from that direction wouldn't be able to see him. Clint would be below him.

Sandy was still on the ground, but now she started to scamper over to him.

"No," he said, "stay away!" But she didn't heed him.

He grabbed her arm and pulled her to the dry wash with him.

"I told you to stay away from me," he scolded her. "They're shooting at me."

"But why?"

"Just because," he said.

"Give me a gun," she said. "I can shoot."

"I'd give you a gun, but I've just got the one."

"There are two of them," she said.

"I know," he said, "one across the road and another one above us."

"We're in a cross fire."

"Yes, but the one above us can't see us now," he explained.

"What are we gonna do?"

"You're going to stay right here," he said, "and I'm going to get us out of this."

"How?"

"I'll have a plan," he told her. "Soon."

She folded her arms and glared at him like an angry mother.

"That's not very comforting."

Ed Presser knew he'd made a mistake, although he'd never admit that to his partner. Clint Adams had found himself some cover that had defeated the cross fire. Presser could not see him now and he waved at Chance to stop firing.

They were going to have to try this again somewhere else.

Hal Chance saw Presser waving at him. The two men had ridden together long enough to be able to interpret each other's hand signals. Presser wanted him to stop and move out. He'd meet him farther ahead with the horses.

Chance left his position, smiling because he knew his partner had made a mistake and would never admit it.

"What's happening?" Sandy asked. "Why aren't they shooting anymore?"

"I think they've realized their mistake," Clint said. "We're not in a cross fire anymore, and that was their advantage."

"So then they're . . . what? Quitting?"

"I think they've done it," he said. "They've quit. They're gone."

"But . . . why?"

He looked at her.

"Any man who would shoot at another man from ambush is a coward," he said. "Now that they've lost their edge they're running."

"Then we can stand up and get out of this hole?" she asked.

He put his hand on her shoulder and shoved her back down.

"I'll stand up and we'll see what happens," he said. "You wait here."

"I'm not afraid," she said.

"I never said you were afraid," he said. "I'm just telling you—asking you—to wait here. Is that all right?"

"That's fine," she said, "but hurry. I don't want the horses to get too far away."

"We'll go and collect the horses as soon as I make sure the shooters are gone."

"Okay," she said, folding her arms again. "And hurry up."

"Yes, ma'am."

EIGHT

The horses had not gone far. Eclipse was too smart to wander away, and Sandy's horse had simply stayed with him. Clint felt sorry for the mare if she had designs on Eclipse, because he was a gelding.

"Are you all right?" he asked, after giving her a lift into the saddle.

"I'm fine, Father," she said. "Can I call you Father?"

"I suppose so," he said.

"If you don't want me to," she said, "if it makes you uncomfortable—"

"No, no, it's fine," he said, patting her on the leg. "Don't worry about it making me uncomfortable. It's just going to take some getting used to."

"I understand."

He mounted up and they started for Kansas City again. He supposed he could have done worse for a daughter. She was smart, and she had kept her cool under fire. She sounded like she'd been to school, but there were enough "ain'ts" and "gonnas" in her speech when she wasn't watching herself that he knew she was trying to impress him.

"Can I ask a question?" she asked. "About the shooting?"

"Of course."

"What if they weren't shooting at you?"

"Why would they be shooting at you, Sandy?"

She shrugged.

"Maybe because they knew I was coming to fetch you," she said. "Bring you back to Kansas City to find my mother's killer."

"How would they know that?"

"I don't know," she said. "I'm just asking a question."

"Well, when we were on the ground the bullets were coming at me," he said, "not you. That was why I was telling you to keep away from me."

She thought a moment, then nodded.

"All right," she said. "You know best about these things."

"Well, thank you," he said.

She turned her head and looked at him.

"I'm sorry if I get . . . bossy," she said. "My aunts tell me I do that just like my mother."

"That's okay," he said. "I can't think of any part of your mother you should be ashamed to have."

She smiled and said, "I can't either."

"You made me walk a mile," Hal Chance complained to Presser.

"We had to get far enough away before meetin' up," Presser said. "Just mount up."

Chance grabbed his horse and swung into the saddle. He knew Presser was mad because he'd made a mistake, and he was taking it out on him.

"What are we gonna do now?"

"We'll ride up ahead," Presser said. "We've still got a lot of miles to go between here and Kansas City. We'll get another chance."

"What happens if we don't get another shot at him?" Chance asked. "What if he makes it to Kansas City?"

"Then we ain't gettin' paid," Presser said. "And we'll be in a whole lot of trouble, so don't even think about that."

"Hey," Chance said, "don't jump down my throat. I was just curious, is all."

"Wait," Clint said.

They reined their horses in.

"What is it?"

"If we stay on this road, we'll give the shooters another chance to ambush us."

"So what should we do?"

"We'll get off the road," Clint said. "Go another way. It may take a little longer, but it'll be safer."

"You think they're still waiting for us up ahead?" she asked.

"For me," he said, "yes."

"Why don't we circle around and ambush them?"

"Well, first of all, I don't ambush people," he said, "and second, I don't want to put you at risk again."

"I told you I'm not scared."

"Maybe you're not," Clint said, "but I've just found out I have a daughter, so I'm too scared to risk your life."

"You're worried about me?" she asked.

"Yes," he said, "I'm worried about you. All I want to do is get you to Kansas City safe and sound. Isn't that what a father should be thinking about?"

"Yes," she said, "yes, it is."

NINE

They reached Kansas City a little later than Clint had planned, but it was still daylight. He hoped the ambushers were still sitting on a hill somewhere, disappointed.

"Were you and your mom living here?" Clint asked as they rode in.

"Yes, we had a house in town."

"What about your aunts?"

"No, they only came when they heard that Mom was—had been shot."

"So where would they be staying?"

She shrugged and said, "With Mom gone and me away, maybe they're at the house."

"Okay, lead the way," he said. "Let's go and check out the house."

They rode through bustling Kansas City, dodging buckboards, coaches and pedestrians all on the go, until they reached a residential area of small, wood-frame houses in various states of repair and disrepair. When Sandy stopped in front of one of them, Clint was happy to see that it was a rather well-appointed, freshly painted two-story affair, with a picket fence that didn't look like a gap-toothed smile.

They dismounted and tied off their horses, and Sandy rushed for the door. She slowed suddenly, though, as if she'd just remembered that her mother was not inside. She turned and waited for Clint to catch up to her.

"Maybe we should knock," Clint said.

"Why?" she asked. "It's my house."

They opened the front door and went in, with Clint behind her.

"Where the hell have you been?" a large blond woman yelled. She grabbed Sandy and pulled her into a huge hug. "We've been worried sick."

It took Clint a while to recognize Sandy Spillane. He remembered her as a robust blonde, not pretty but with an earthy, sexy appeal. Now she seemed to have gained thirty pounds and while she still wore a man's shirt and jeans, the clothing seemed to be bursting at the seams. Her hair, golden blond in his memory, was now a sort of dull grayish blond. It hadn't been all that long since he'd seen her, but it didn't look as if the years had been kind to her.

"Clint?" she said, eyeing him. "Is that you?"

"It's me, Sandy."

"My God," she said, "the child did it."

"Did what?"

"Katy and I wondered if she'd find you."

She released Sandy and came to Clint, enveloped him in a somewhat less desperate hug.

"It's been years," she said. "You haven't changed."

"You look good, Sandy," he said, holding her at arm's length. *Son of a bitch*, he thought, *if she didn't still have that sexy quality to her.*

"Liar," she said. "I've gained weight since I stopped making my living on a horse."

"Where's Katy?" he asked.

"She's in town, she'll be back soon," the big blonde replied. "Did Sandy tell you?"

"Yes, she did," he said. "I'm so sorry . . ."

"She talked about you, at the end," Sandy said.

Clint rubbed his hand over his face and said, "Well, that doesn't make me feel any better."

"I'm sorry," she said, "I didn't mean—"

"There are two horses out front," Katy Littlefeather called as she entered the house. "Is Sandy . . . Clint? Is that you?"

"Hello, Katy."

Katy Littlefeather hadn't changed a bit. She still looked young and beautiful, except that she was wearing white man's clothes instead of her Indian garb.

She was holding a couple of packages in her hands and set them down on a chair so she could hug him.

"It's so good to see you," she said, her voice catching.

"I'm so sorry," he said, hugging her tightly.

"I know."

They held the embrace for a few seconds more, and then Katy pulled back, wiped her face with the heels of her hands and asked, "So what do you think of our Little Sandy?"

"Don't call me that," the girl said.

"Hey," Sandy Spillane said, "as long as I'm Big Sandy you'll be Little Sandy. Live with it."

The girl frowned but Clint could tell this was comfortable banter for her.

"She's something," Clint said. "I'm very impressed with her."

Little Sandy's face blushed bright red and she turned away to hide it.

They all stood around then, as if they didn't quite know what the next move was.

"Let me help you take those packages into the kitchen," Big Sandy said.

"Okay." Katy picked up the packages and Big Sandy awkwardly took one from her.

"C-can I help—" Clint started.

"No, no, I'll make some coffee, Clint, and then we can talk," Sandy said over her shoulder.

"Okay."

As her aunts left the room, Little Sandy said, "You got them all nervous."

"It's been a while," Clint said.

"Why don't you sit down?" she said. "I'm gonna go in my room and change into some clean clothes."

"Fine," Clint said.

After Little Sandy left and he was alone in the room, Clint realized he'd been feeling a little nervous, too, about seeing Big Sandy and Katy again. Or maybe they were all just nervous to be talking about Anne Archer.

Other than being embarrassed when Clint said he was impressed with her, the teenage girl seemed to be the one who was the least uncomfortable with the situation.

TEN

When coffee was ready the women offered to bring it into the living room, but Clint suggested they all just sit in the kitchen. When the four of them were situated at the table with cups in front of them—little Sandy apparently liked coffee, and liked it strong—somebody finally brought up the subject.

"Do they know who killed her?" Clint asked.

"They say no," Sandy Spillane said.

"They say no?" Clint repeated. "But you don't believe them?"

She looked at Katy, and Katy looked at Little Sandy. To her credit the young girl did not look away, but stared back at her aunt with a look that said, "Well?"

"Clint . . ." Sandy Spillane said, then looked at Sandy.

"I think Sandy has a right to hear whatever you have to say about her mother," Clint offered.

"She's only fifteen . . ." Sandy said, helplessly.

"Almost sixteen," Clint said, before the other Sandy could correct her aunt.

"All right," Sandy said, "almost sixteen. We think we know who killed Anne."

"What?" Little Sandy said. "You know who killed my mother? Why hasn't he been arrested?"

"She said we think we know, Sandy," Katy said. "We can't prove it."

"Why not?" Clint asked. "Go to the police and let them prove it."

"They wouldn't want to," Sandy said.

"Wouldn't want to prove it?" Clint asked. "I don't understand."

"I don't either," Little Sandy said.

"There's a lot of money in play here," Sandy said. "The man we have in mind is rich, and . . ."

"Oh, I get it," Clint said.

"I still don't," the young girl said. "What has him being rich have to do with anything?"

"It has everything to do with everything," Clint said. "Rich and powerful people think they can get away with anything, Sandy."

"Like killing my mother?"

"Like anything," Sandy Spillane said.

"But Clint . . . Father," Sandy said, "you're not going to let that happen, are you?"

"No," Clint said, "no, Sandy, I'm not about to let that happen." He looked at the two women. "Tell me who it is we're talking about?"

It was after dark when Ed Presser and Hal Chance came riding into Kansas City, knowing that they had somehow messed things up. Adams and the girl must have gone around and gotten to Kansas City ahead of them. Now Presser was going to have to explain that to his boss.

"You know," Hal Chance said as they rode into town, "for once I'm glad you're the brains of this outfit."

"Shut up," Presser said wearily.

"We gave up bounty hunting a while back," Sandy said, "but we're not completely out of it."

"It?" Clint asked. "What's it?"

"The excitement," Katy said.

"The thrill of the hunt," Sandy Spillane said.

"Ladies, just what are you trying to tell me?" Clint asked.

"Clint," Sandy said, "we're Pinkertons."

Clint sat back in his chair and blinked.

ELEVEN

"What? When did that happen?"

"About five years ago," Katy said. "We were on a job, and met Allan Pinkerton. When the job was over, he offered us positions as detectives."

"Well," Clint said, "I've got to give it to ol' Allan. He's smart."

"That's right," Sandy said, "you know him."

"We're acquainted," Clint said.

"What does this all mean?" Little Sandy asked.

"Yes," Clint said, "what does it mean?"

"We're investigating Colonel Louis G. Cameron," Sandy said. "He's a banker here in town, and he's heavy into politics. In fact, he's trying to get his son, William, into the U.S. Senate."

"So you're after the father?"

"The father, the son," Sandy said, "the whole family, if we can get them."

"The women, too?"

"Well," Katy said, "the son's wife. His mother is dead."

"And there's a stepmother," Big Sandy said. "Who's kind of young."

"Ick," Little Sandy said. "She married an old man?"

"Some women do that," Clint said, "for money."

"Ick, but she'd have to let him touch her."

"Some women do that, too," Sandy Spillane said.

"So you think Cameron had her killed, or the son had her killed, or somebody in their circle had her killed."

"Or William did it himself," Sandy Spillane said. "Anne told us she had found the evidence we needed to put them all away."

"Don't tell me, let me guess," Clint said. "None of you know where this evidence is."

"Anne thought we'd all be safer that way," Sandy Spillane said. "I think she was worried about Little Sandy getting involved."

"Wait," Little Sandy said. "My mother got killed because she was trying to protect me?"

"That's not certain," Katy said. "We won't know until we find out who killed her and why."

"Why was Anne living here and the two of you weren't?" Clint asked.

"She was undercover, working for the Cameron family," Katy explained. "She got to know them."

Katy looked Little Sandy's way and Clint decided that this time whatever they were trying to keep from the young girl was better kept secret.

"I'm kind of beat," he said suddenly. "I think I should check into a hotel—"

"No, no," Little Sandy said, grabbing his arm, "you have to stay here."

He put his hand over hers and said, "If I'm going to find out who killed your mother, Sandy, I'll be better off in town."

"Then I'll come and stay with you."

"No, you stay here with your aunts," Clint said. "I need to be able to move around."

"Honey, why don't you go out and take care of the horse you, uh, borrowed," Sandy Spillane said.

"I have to take it back."

"You can do that tomorrow," she said. "We arranged for you not to be arrested."

"I'm sorry," Little Sandy said, "I just had to go and find Father."

"Well," Katy said, "you found him, and it was probably a good idea. Go ahead, take care of the horse."

"I'll say good night, Sandy."

The young girl stood and asked, "Will I see you tomorrow?"

"Definitely."

He stood and she came around the table to hug him. He held her tightly, then kissed the top of her head.

"Good night, Sandy."

"'Night, Father."

She went out the back door, presumably to go around the house and collect the horse.

"Now, what didn't you want to say in front of Little Sandy?" Clint asked.

"Bill Cameron and Anne were . . . seeing each other," Sandy said.

"He was cheating on his wife with her?"

"That's right."

"So that makes the wife a good suspect."

"Yes," Katy said, "that's what we thought. Or, if it's about the evidence, then it was the father or son, or someone working for them."

"Okay," Clint said. "That gives me somewhere to start."

"Gives you somewhere?" Sandy asked. "We're the Pinkertons. Now that you're here, and because you're Sandy's father, you can assist but—"

"I tell you what," Clint said. "Why don't we talk more about this tomorrow?"

"Why tomorrow?"

"Because I want to argue about this," Clint said, "but I don't want to argue with the two of you tonight."

They both stared at him, then their eyes filled with tears. He hugged them both and had to get out of there before he made a fool of himself.

"You're telling me you missed?" Louis G. Cameron asked Ed Presser.

"Yes, sir."

"What did I pay you and that idiot partner of yours for, Presser?"

"I know, sir—"

"So Clint Adams is in Kansas City now?"

"I don't know, sir—"

"You don't know, Presser?" The wealthy man's rage was barely suppressed. He sat behind his desk, holding on to his gold-tipped cane. Presser had seen him inflict much damage with that cane, and he kept his eyes on it.

"I suggest you find out," Cameron said. "Find out if he's in town, and where he is."

"Yes, sir," Presser said. "And when I do that, should we kill him?"

"You had your chance, Presser," Cameron said. "I believe if you and your idiot partner tried again, the Gunsmith would surely kill both of you. No, I shall go elsewhere now for my talent, and I will keep in mind that you get what you pay for in this life."

"Yes, sir."

"Get out," Cameron said. "Don't come back until you find him. And if you don't find him, don't come back."

"Yes, sir."

As Presser went out the door, Cameron was tempted to take his gun from his desk drawer and shoot the man in the back. He'd terminated a man's employment that way more than once. It was very satisfying.

When the office door opened again, his wife, Olivia, came in. She was thirty-four years younger than he was and breathtakingly beautiful. She'd agreed to marry him on the condition that he never try to touch her. It had only been a year so far, but he'd kept his promise.

"Did they find him?"

"Found him and missed him."

Olivia came around behind Cameron and put her hands on his shoulders.

"And you let him walk out alive?"

"He'll locate him," Cameron said, "and then I'll have someone else kill him."

"Like who?"

Cameron gestured with his cane.

"For a man of my wealth the answer is, anyone I want."

TWELVE

Clint had been to Kansas City before, though not in a while. He still knew the way to one of the best hotels in town. If he was going to be rubbing elbows with the rich and elite of Kansas City, he had to appear as if he belonged with them. That meant staying at the Kansas City Plaza.

He dismounted in front of the hotel and a man approached him. He was wearing what looked like a military uniform, but he was just a glorified doorman.

"Will you be staying, sir?" the man asked.

"I will."

"Can we take care of your horse?"

"If you have somebody who can handle him," Clint said. "My name's Adams. If you can't find anybody, I'll come back down and do it."

"Fine lookin' animal, sir," the doorman said. "We have a good horseman workin' for us. He'll handle him."

"If he does manage to handle my horse," Clint said, "I'll be interested in meeting him later."

"I'll tell him."

Clint gave the man a dollar and went inside.

"Hello, sir," the desk clerk said. "Checking in?"

"I hope so."

"Do you have a reservation?"

"No," Clint said, "that's why I said I hope so."

"Well . . ."

"I'm in town to do business with Mr. Cameron."

"Louis Cameron?"

"Any Cameron," Clint said. "I'm actually here to do business with the family."

"And your name?"

"Clint Adams."

"Oh . . . Mr. Adams? Well, of course, I'm sure we can accommodate you."

"Since I'll be doing business with the Cameron family, I'll need a room I can entertain them in."

"Of course," the man said. "Will a suite do?"

"Yes," Clint said, "one with a view of the front street."

"Yes," the clerk said, "I have just the room. Do you have any luggage?"

"Just these," Clint said, indicating his saddlebags. "I travel light and buy what I need when I get there."

"Of course, sir. Will you sign the register, please?" He turned the book toward Clint and fetched a key while he signed it.

"Thank you, sir. Here is your key. Suite Two, on the second floor."

"Thank you." Clint started away, then turned back. "Oh, I could use a bath."

"Yes, sir. I'll have the water brought to your room right away."

"In the morning is good enough," Clint said. "Eight A.M.?"

"Yes, sir," the clerk said. "Sharp."

"Thank you."

"Good night, sir."

Clint went up the stairs to the second floor, found Suite Two and let himself in. The suite was impressive but he only gave it a glance on his way to the window. The view outside was lit up by street lamps, but most of the light was coming from the Red Garter Saloon and Dance Hall across the street.

Clint knew that upstairs the Red Garter provided gambling—both house games and private ones. He had a good night there once, walked out with twenty-five thousand from a private game.

But he wasn't in Kansas City to gamble or watch dancing girls. He could use a drink, though, so he left the room, went downstairs and crossed the street to the Red Garter.

After Clint went upstairs, the desk clerk pulled out a piece of paper, wrote a note and waved to a black porter.

"Take this over to Mr. Cameron's office," he said. "See that his personal assistant gets it. No one else. Understood?"

"Yassuh."

"Go, and hurry back. I have work for you."

"Yassuh."

The porter hurried out the front door.

When Clint Adams reappeared moments later, the desk clerk was startled, but he simply nodded and smiled as the man went past him and out the door. Then the clerk breathed a sigh of relief.

The porter found his way to the large brick building that housed Louis G. Cameron and all his various endeavors.

It took some talking but he finally got past the front van-
guard and was allowed to see Mr. Walters, Mr. Cameron's
personal assistant.

"The desk clerk over ta the Plaza tol' me to give this to
nobody but you, suh."

"Is that right?"

Walters took the note from the porter's hand, using the
tips of his forefinger and thumb, trying to touch the note
as little as possible. He finally opened and read it, then
nodded.

"Thank you." He gave the porter a nickel.

"Thank ya, suh," the porter said, and left.

Walters put the note down on the desk, removed his
handkerchief and used it to wipe the slip of paper clean.
Then and only then did he pick it up and carry it into his
boss's office. It was late, but all the Camerons kept late
hours. In fact, Mr. Cameron's wife was still with him
when Walters entered. She was helping him get his coat
on, so they were apparently ready to quit for the day.

"Can that wait until tomorrow, Walters?" Olivia asked.

"Uh, no, ma'am, I don't think it can."

"Oh, leave Walters alone, he's just doing his job,"
Cameron said. "Bring it here, man."

Cameron extended a liver-spotted hand to Walters who
held the note out, careful not to touch the old man's hand.

"Cleaned it off, did you?" Cameron asked, chuckling.

"Yes, sir, as best I could."

"You and your germs. Who's it from?"

"The desk clerk at the Plaza, sir."

Cameron read the note, then started to laugh.

"Something funny, dear?" Olivia asked.

"Yes, love," he said, "that's why I'm laughing." He
gave Walters a look that said, "Stupid woman."

"Walters, in the morning please get in touch with Ed Presser and tell him that his services will no longer be necessary."

"Yes, sir."

"Then get ahold of Joseph Bravo and have him meet me here at eleven A.M."

"Yes, sir." Walters didn't ask what would happen if he could not locate Joe Bravo by that time. He just would.

"Very good. Mrs. Cameron and I are going home now. You lock up."

"Yes, sir."

Cameron headed for the door, unaware that behind him, as Olivia passed Walter, she reached out and brushed her hand across his crotch. He seemed to forget all about his phobia for germs when they were in bed together.

THIRTEEN

When Clint entered the saloon he squinted, his senses assailed by all the red. He'd forgotten the "Red" in Red Garter referred to more than just the name of the place. All the lampshades were red, as was the flocked paper on the walls. Even the bar was red mahogany. He wondered if the place was still owned and run by the same man, Tommy Turner.

The bar was long, as had become the norm in places like this, and there was plenty of room for him to find a spot to signal the bartender.

"Beer," he said.

"Comin' up."

The place was alive with activity, girls dancing on a stage in the front, other girls working the floor, men yelling and banging on the tables, drinking, smoking and getting rowdy, like they were supposed to.

When the bartender brought the beer back, Clint asked, "Tommy Turner still own this place?"

"Oh, yeah," the man said, "owns it and runs it. You a friend of his?"

"Acquaintance," Clint said. "I played poker upstairs one time."

"What's your name?"

"Clint Adams."

The bartender snapped his fingers.

"Twenty-five grand, right?"

"That's right," Clint said. "You have a good memory."

"Oh, I wasn't workin' here then, but I heard the story," the barkeeps said. "You took it off Luke Short, Ben Thompson and some others."

"I didn't realize it was a story," Clint said.

"Hey, I'll tell the boss you're here," the man said. "Maybe he can get a game up for ya."

"That's okay," Clint said. "Tell him I'm here, by all means, but I'm not here to play poker this time. Got other business."

"Well, if ya change your mind he'll do it for ya," the man said. "My name's Roscoe, and I'll let 'im know you're here."

"Thanks, Roscoe."

"And I'm sure he'll want that beer to be on the house."

"Thanks."

Clint enjoyed the cold beer, turned his back to the bar so he could lean against it and survey the room. A picture of Anne Archer suddenly rushed into his mind, red hair, full moist lips, a smile that could light up the night. *Years wasted*, he thought . . .

He turned his mind to the business at hand. All three women were Pinkerton detectives. If the Cameron family was responsible for Anne's death, it was entirely possible they knew about Sandy and Katy as well.

As if on cue Sandy Spillane walked through the batwings. A big, solid blonde, she commanded the attention of the men in the place, and not only because of the gun she wore on her hip.

She scanned the room, spotted Clint and started over to him. A man who was half-drunk and should have known better sauntered toward her, leaned over and whispered something into her ear. Then he paid the price when Sandy elbowed him in the stomach hard enough to double him over and stomped on his toe before moving away. The man's friends came over and, laughing, helped him to a chair.

"Beer?" Clint asked.

"Please."

Clint signaled to Roscoe, who nodded and hurried over with a full mug.

"The lady a friend of yours?" he asked.

Clint wondered if the point was to find out if Sandy was a lady unescorted in a saloon.

"Yes."

"Then she drinks on the house, too."

Sandy grabbed her beer and said to Clint, "You make friends fast."

"I've been here before," he said. "Apparently, there's a story going around . . ." He left it at that. "Where's Katy?"

"She's at the house with Sandy," she said. "She won't go to sleep, so Katy's sitting up, talking with her."

"That's some kid," he said. "I can see Anne in her."

"A lot of Anne is in her," Sandy said, "but you don't see any of you in her?"

"No," he said, "not yet."

"She's as stubborn as you are."

"That could've come from Anne."

"That's true," she said.

"Are you here for a beer and to do damage to the male population?"

"I came here looking for you."

"What's on your mind?"

"That's what I was going to ask you," she said. "I thought you might have some questions you couldn't ask in front of Little Sandy."

"Really," he said, "I can see why she hates that name."

"What else would you have us call her?" she asked. "I didn't ask Annie to name her after me."

"I don't know," he said. "I'll give it some thought."

"You do that and get back to me."

Her tone was almost angry, and he realized she was mad at her friend for getting killed.

He understood. He'd lost many friends over the years, and too early. He was mad at all of them.

FOURTEEN

"You know," she said, thoughtfully, "she changed the least of us all."

"What do you mean?"

"I mean physically," she said. "Look at me, put on weight. And Katy, she's still pretty, but Annie? She stayed radiant. That was why we thought she was the one to go undercover. We knew that Bill Cameron loved beautiful women."

"Is his wife beautiful?"

"Very."

"Then why cheat?"

"Are you sure you're a man?" she asked. "Not some mythical creature? Men cheat, it doesn't matter how wonderful they have it at home. They cheat. It's in them. They're men."

"Okay," he said, "I get it. Men cheat."

"She didn't set out to actually sleep with him, but . . . entice him a little, you know?"

"She didn't actually . . ."

"What?"

"You know . . . fall for him?"

"Hell, no," she said. "It was all business for her. You were the only man for her, Clint."

"Okay, don't—"

"I'm sorry if you don't like hearing it, but it's true," she said. "She would've quit for you, settled down . . ."

"We would have been miserable."

"Probably," Sandy said, "but she would've done it. All you had to do was ask."

"I couldn't."

"She knew that," Sandy said, "and understood."

"And you and Katy?" Clint asked. "Do you understand?"

"No," she said. "We both think you're a bastard for letting her go . . . but we still love you."

"So if I hadn't let her go, and I had asked her to settle down, she'd probably still be alive."

"Well, if you're gonna think that way you're really gonna tear yourself up inside."

"Tell me about . . . when she got pregnant."

"It was hard on her," Sandy said. "She knew it was yours. She hadn't been with anyone else. We wanted her to tell you, but she wouldn't. She said that would be trapping you."

"And the last time we all saw each other, Sandy had already been born?" Clint asked.

"Oh, hell, she was what? Five or six at that time? Annie made us promise not to tell you anything. It was hard, but we kept our promise." She laughed. "That little girl was a firecracker when she was young. You would've loved her."

"It would have been nice to have had the chance . . ."

"So what about this?" she asked.

"What about what?"

"Katy and I are working on finding out exactly how Annie was killed."

"Where did it happen?"

"Right on the street, out there," Sandy said. "Shot in the back from ambush."

"Goddamnit!" Cowards made him livid. He'd lost his best friend Wild Bill Hickok to a coward's bullet.

"Two bullets in the back and she still lasted long enough to ask for us, and for Sandy, and to tell her daughter about her father. It was if she just refused to die until she did that."

"That stubbornness."

"Yeah."

Both their mugs were empty.

"You want another one?" he asked.

"One more and then I have to get back."

Clint called Roscoe over and told him to bring two more beers.

"I'll pay for these," he added.

"Whatever you say."

Roscoe brought them and took Clint's money.

"So tell me about the Camerons."

"The old man controls a lot of what goes on in Kansas City, a fair amount of what happens in Missouri, and some of what happens in Washington, D.C."

"That much power?"

"That much."

"What about the son?"

"Billy Boy is the apple of Daddy's eye," Sandy said. "Wants him to follow in Daddy's footsteps."

"And how does Billy Boy feel about that?"

"According to Annie, Billy wasn't happy about his father pulling his strings. He wanted to dance to his own tune."

"So he was rebellious?"

"A little, but he was too afraid of his father to try very hard."

"Where does he go?" Clint asked. "What does he do?"

"He goes where his father tells him to go, and does what he tells him to do."

"And where did he go when he was trying to break the strings?"

"He used to take Annie to this saloon across town," Sandy said. "That was where he went when he wanted to drink, to get away from Daddy."

"Give me the name," Clint said.

"Clint, I told you that Katy and I—"

"Has it occurred to you that if they knew about Annie they'd know about you and Katy, too?"

She hesitated, then said, "It has occurred to us, yes."

"I think you and Katy should go someplace, and take Sandy with you. Leave this to me."

"Clint—"

"I'm sure Annie did all she could," he said. "Maybe there are some things only a man can do."

"I hate to admit it," she said, "but maybe there is."

FIFTEEN

Clint insisted on walking Sandy back to the house. But before they could leave the saloon, a well-dressed man appeared, a smile on his lined face.

"Clint Adams, as I live and breathe."

Clint turned and said, "Tommy, is that you? You're looking very prosperous."

Tommy Turner patted his corpulent belly and said, "If by that you mean well-fed, then yes, I plead guilty. How the hell are you?"

The two men shook hands and Clint introduced Turner to Sandy.

"It's a pleasure, ma'am. Has Roscoe been takin' good care of the both of you?"

"Roscoe's been great, Tommy, thanks," Clint said.

"He told me you weren't in town lookin' for a game," Turner said. "Sure I couldn't persuade you?"

"I tell you what, Tommy. Hold that thought. I've got to walk Sandy home—"

"I can get home by myself just fine, Clint," she said, cutting him off. She looked at Turner. "Sometimes he's just too much of a gentlemen."

"Well, I must say the lady looks like she can take care of herself, Clint."

"Ask Charlie Rosen, over there," Roscoe chimed in from behind the bar. "He's still feelin' the effects."

"Charlie Rosen is always feelin' the effects of somethin'," Turner said. "I tell you what, Clint. I'll have Roscoe walk her home, and he'll carry his scattergun. How's that?"

"Look, I don't need—"

"It'd be my pleasure, ma'am," Roscoe said. "And I could sure use the air."

"Well . . . fine."

Roscoe grabbed his shotgun from beneath the bar, came around and said, "Lead the way, ma'am."

"Stop callin' me ma'am," Sandy said. "My name is Sandy." She looked at Clint. "I'll see you tomorrow."

"Good night, Sandy."

"Let's go, barkeep," she said. "See if you can keep up."

"Let me get you another beer," Turner said as Sandy and Roscoe went out the door. Turner obviously had a well-trained staff, because there was already another man behind the bar.

"That's okay, Tommy," Clint said. "I was thinking we'd go to your office and have a talk."

"This sounds serious. Follow me."

Turner led Clint through the Red Garter, glad-handing as he went, fielding some questions from staff, until they finally reached a door in the back of the room. Turner used a key to open it and they stepped into a small but very well-appointed office.

"Back here I can offer you brandy or whiskey," Turner said.

"Nothing, thanks."

"Then have a seat and tell me what's on your mind, Clint."

They sat across from each other with Turner's mahogany desk between them.

"There's a family named Cameron in town," Clint said.

"You mean there's a family named Cameron who owns the town," Turner said.

"How can somebody own Kansas City?" Clint asked. "And why didn't I hear about this last time I was here?"

"Last time you were here you were involved in a three-day poker game," Turner said. "You didn't notice anything else—except, maybe, Irene, my best girl."

"Oh, yeah, Irene," Clint said. "She still here?"

Turner shook his head.

"Left a short time after you did. To answer your other question, you have to have a big reputation, a lot of money and unlimited power. And it doesn't hurt to have a sheriff, a marshal, a judge and some U.S. senators in your pocket."

Clint rubbed his jaw.

"I don't know that I've ever come up against somebody with that much power."

"Probably not," Turner said. "Some folks think he's more powerful than the president."

Clint frowned.

"That's not a happy look," Turner said. "What's your interest?"

"I think this family may have killed a friend of mine."

"Who? And when?"

"Her name was Anne Archer, and it happened earlier this month."

"Oh, that woman," Turner said. "I read about that. Rumor has it she was seeing Bill Cameron."

"What else do the rumors say?"

"Not much," Turner said. "It was good for one day in the papers, and a couple of days of rumors, and then it faded. She wasn't really . . ."

"Anybody?" Clint asked. "Is that what you were about to say?"

"Look, I'm sorry your friend was killed," Turner said. "If there's anything I can do . . ."

"What if I told you I'm going to find out who did it and make them pay?" Clint asked. "What if I said I don't care which member of the family it was? Would you want to help me then?"

"Look, Clint," Turner said, squirming, "I've got to make a living in this city—and we are a city, we're not really a town anymore. And the Camerons are a big reason for that."

"Okay," Clint said, "I'm not going to ask you to help, just answer a few questions."

Turner looked relieved.

"I'll do what I can."

"Who's the law around here?"

"We've got Sheriff Hardesty," Turner said. "He's firmly in Cameron's pocket."

"And?"

"We've got a modern police force now, headed up by Chief of Police Dan Fortune."

"And is Fortune in Cameron's pocket?"

"I don't think so," Turner said. "But I'm sure a few key members of his department are."

"Where's Fortune from?"

"San Francisco," Turner said. "He was a policeman there, a lieutenant, I think. Interviewed for this job and got it. A lot of people are not happy with him, specifically the Camerons."

"Because he doesn't fit in their pocket?"

"Doesn't, or won't."

Clint stood up.

"He sounds like the man I want to see. Thanks, Tommy."

"No hard feelings, huh, Clint?" Turner asked, also standing.

"No, Tommy," Clint said, "but if I find out you went to the Camerons, there will be."

"Hey," Turner said, "why would I do that?"

"Power makes people do funny things," Clint said, "especially the people who don't have it. I'll be seeing you, Tommy."

SIXTEEN

It was too late to visit the chief of police, so Clint went across the street to his hotel and to his room to get some sleep. He was in his room five minutes when there was a knock on the door. Since he hadn't had time to take his gun off, he palmed it and went to the door.

"Who is it?"

"Porter, suh."

"I didn't ask for anything."

"I got somethin' for ya anyway, suh. Please open the door."

Clint cracked the door, saw the black porter standing in the hall, then opened it.

"Quick, let me in," the man said, ducking in.

"Is there something I can do for you?" Clint asked.

"Yes, close the door," the man said in perfect English. "Quickly."

Clint closed the door, then turned to face the man.

"Look, I know you don't know me," the man said. "Around here I go by the name Leon."

"That's not your real name?"

"No," Leon said, "but it will do."

"Okay, Leon, why the act? Your English is obviously better than you used out in the hall . . . suh."

"You don't need that gun."

"I'll be the judge of that."

Leon was wearing a waistcoat, tight trousers and shoes with a high black shine.

"This is what they make me wear here," he said, "and there's no place to hide a gun."

"Keep talking," Clint said, maintaining hold of his gun.

"Mr. Adams, I know who you are, and you should know that not ten minutes after you checked in, the desk clerk—his name is Rawlins, by the way—sent me over to Mr. Cameron with a message."

"What kind of message?"

"Just that you were here, checked into this hotel."

"Why would that interest Mr. Cameron?"

"Everything interests Mr. Cameron."

"We talking about Louis Cameron?"

"He's the only one who counts."

"And why are you telling me this?"

"I'm warning you, that's all."

"You could've kept up your mush-mouthed act for that," Clint said.

"I guess I just wanted you to know that's not who I am."

"And if it's not, then why are you pretending that's who you are."

"That's too complicated for now, and I've got to get back downstairs. I just thought you should know."

"Well, I'm obliged, I guess, but I'd like to talk about it a little more."

"I'll leave you a note, tell you where to meet me tomorrow. We can talk then."

"Maybe you can help me—"

"And maybe you can help me," Leon said, "but we'll have to talk about it tomorrow."

Leon moved quickly to the door, opened it, stuck his head out, then slipped away, leaving Clint standing there holding his gun, wondering what had just happened.

He holstered the gun, removed the holster and hung it on the bedpost, where it always resided when he was in a hotel. He walked to the window and looked down at the street. Somebody had tried to bushwhack him on the way here. He'd assumed it was someone who recognized him in St. Jo, but now he wasn't so sure. Had Sandy been right? Had they been after her? Or both of them? And was the point to keep him from Kansas City?

And who but the Cameron family would want that?

SEVENTEEN

Clint slept fitfully, which was odd because the bed was one of the best he'd ever slept in. He dreamt all night about Anne Archer, and about Little Sandy, and how they were a family living on a ranch somewhere, only to have men invade their home to make a try at the Gunsmith's reputation. Every dream ended up with Clint alive, standing over the bodies of the invaders and his family. All dead but him.

He woke for the final time when the sun streamed in his window and quit the bed. He didn't want to take a chance on having another dream.

A knock on the door sent him grabbing for his gun, but it was a porter—not Leon—with the water for the bath he'd forgotten he ordered.

Once the bathtub was filled with hot water, he shaved, then soaked in the tub until the water was tepid. Next he dressed but quickly realized he had nothing with him that fit Kansas City and the company he was going to end up keeping. That meant some shopping—but not until after breakfast.

* * *

Clint brought his new purchases back to the hotel and asked the desk clerk to have a porter take them up to his room.

"Of course, sir."

The clerk waved and the porter who came over was Leon, the black man who had come to his room.

"Yassuh?"

"Take these things up to Mr. Adams's room."

"Yassuh."

Leon never looked Clint's way, so Clint did the man the courtesy of returning the favor. The black man picked up the packages and made his way up the stairs to the second floor.

Clint started to leave, but decided to give the desk clerk something to think about—or rather, something to take back to Louis Cameron.

"Can you give me directions to the police station, please?"

"Sir?"

"You do have a police department in town, don't you?" Clint asked innocently.

"Well, yes, sir, but if there's a problem I'm sure the sheriff could help you."

"I think I'd rather take it to the chief of police," Clint said. "Directions?"

"Uh, yes, sir," the clerk said and provided them in detail.

"Thank you."

"Uh, sir?"

"Yes."

"There's no problem here—I mean, with the hotel? Nothing . . . missing from your room, or anything like that?"

"No," Clint said, "nothing like that. It's a more . . . personal matter."

"I see."

"But thank you for the concern."

"Uh, yes, sir, we do, uh, try to keep our guests . . . happy."

"And you're doing a bang up job of it, too." Clint actually leaned over and patted the man on the shoulder. "Keep it up."

"Uh, yes, sir. Thank you, sir."

Clint nodded and left the hotel. Maybe that would give the desk clerk and Louis Cameron something to think about.

EIGHTEEN

The police station was a modern, two-story brick structure that dominated the block it was on. Clint entered the building and presented himself at the oversized front desk.

"Yes, sir, what can I do for you this fine day?" the granite-jawed, gray-haired sergeant asked.

"I'd like to see the chief of police, please."

"Well, the chief is a very busy man, sir," the sergeant said. "Maybe there's something I can help you with?"

"Do you know anything about the murder of Anne Archer?" I asked.

"Anne who?" The man screwed up his face. "Murder?"

"I really think I should speak to—"

"Sergeant," a man standing nearby said, "I'll handle this."

"Very well, sir," the sergeant said. "This is Lieutenant Abernathy, sir. He'll take care—"

"Yes, Sergeant O' Connor," Abernathy said, "I just said I'd do that. Please, sir. Over here."

Clint walked over and joined the man, who put his hand out.

"Edgar Abernathy, detective lieutenant."

"Clint Adams."

The two men shook hands. Abernathy appeared to be in his mid-forties, a little taller than Clint, in good shape and wearing a suit that had once been expensive but had seen better days.

"Adams? The Gunsmith? That Clint Adams?"

"That's right."

"And you're here about the Anne Archer case?"

"That's right," Clint said. "At least you know about it."

"I should, I'm working on it."

"Still?"

"Well, I haven't found a killer yet," Abernathy said. "I don't usually close a case until I do that."

"Well, that's good to hear," Clint said.

"Why? Had you heard differently?"

"In fact, yes," Clint said.

"Maybe we should take this to my office," Abernathy said.

"And what about seeing the chief?"

"I'll introduce you after we've talked. Is that all right?"

"Sounds fair enough."

As Clint walked away with Lieutenant Abernathy, Sergeant O'Connor called a young officer over and said, "I've got a message for you to deliver, laddie."

In the lieutenant's office Abernathy closed the door and

sat behind his desk. His office was cramped and his chair hit the wall as he pushed it back.

"Sorry," he said, "they put me in this closet in the hopes that I'd resign."

Clint couldn't tell if the man was being funny or candid. He sat in the rickety chair across from the detective.

"What's your interest in this case, Mr. Adams?" the lieutenant asked.

"The deceased was a friend of mine," Clint said. "A very good friend."

"I see."

"Maybe you do, and maybe you don't," Clint said. "I heard about her murder and I'm here to find out who did it—no matter who it is."

"And what did you mean when you said you were glad to hear I was still working the case?"

"Are we speaking frankly?" Clint asked.

Abernathy smirked and said, "I always speak frankly, Mr. Adams. That's why I'm in this closet."

"I heard that since the Cameron family was involved, there wasn't much being done to solve the case."

Abernathy frowned.

"I was afraid that might be the public's perception," he said, "simply because I haven't caught the killer yet. Believe me, sir, it hasn't been for lack of trying."

"I am going to believe you, Lieutenant," Clint said, "since we're speaking frankly."

"What are your intentions if you find the killer?" the lieutenant asked.

"You know my reputation."

"I don't believe everything I hear or read, sir," Abernathy said.

"I plan to see that Anne Archer's death is avenged," Clint said. "If not for me, then for her daughter's sake."

Abernathy tapped his forefinger on the desk for a few moments as he regarded Clint.

"I'm going to trust you with something, Mr. Adams," he finally said, "if only because this case has frustrated me to no end."

"Okay."

"Of course we know that Miss Archer was seeing Bill Cameron," he said. "I do believe that someone in the family is responsible for her death. For that reason no one is talking to me."

"I've heard all about them since I came to town," Clint commented, "so I can understand that."

"There isn't anyone in this town who isn't afraid of Louis Cameron."

"You're not."

Abernathy smirked.

"Actually, I am, but that won't stop me from arresting him if he did it."

"Who would stop you?"

"Maybe the chief."

"I heard he was his own man, not in Cameron's pocket the way the sheriff is."

Abernathy frowned. "How long you been in town?"

"Got here yesterday evening."

"You're well informed, already."

"I'm going to be honest with you, Lieutenant, and show you just how well informed I am—and hope it goes no further than this."

"That would be refreshing."

"Anne Archer was a Pinkerton."

Abernathy sat straight up in his chair as if a bolt of lightning had gone through his body.

NINETEEN

"What?"

"You didn't know?"

"Not a clue," the lieutenant said, "and you don't know how much that annoys me. I imagine I'm pretty good at this job."

"I'll bet you're right."

"Not if I didn't know that," he said. "How did you know about it?"

"I told you, we were friends."

Abernathy studied Clint for a few moments.

"Bullshit," he said. "You're not being totally honest with me."

"I'm being completely honest."

"Then you're not being totally informative."

"There's a difference."

"She has a partner here in Kansas City."

Clint remained silent.

"You're not working for Pinkerton, are you?"

"No," Clint said, "Ol' Allan and I are not a good fit."

Abernathy laughed.

"You turned him down," he said. "He'd hate that."

"Then we have something in common. You turned him down, too, didn't you?"

Abernathy nodded.

"I prefer to stay official."

"So where do we stand?" Clint asked. "I came over here to feel the chief out, see if I would be able to depend on him and his police department for some help."

"I'll let you speak to the chief and be your own judge," Abernathy said. "As for me, if you get anything I can use, I'd be obliged for it. And since our goal is the same, I'm here to help you if and when you need it."

"That sounds like what I need," Clint said, "but I still want to meet the chief."

"Let's do that now," Abernathy said. "Maybe later we can meet away from here and talk again." He stood up and came around his desk. "Maybe you can talk to the Archer woman's partner and see if they want to come forward on this, as well."

"My concern there is for her daughter," Clint said. He decided not to mention that Sandy was his daughter. If word ever got out that she was the Gunsmith's daughter, her life wouldn't be worth a plugged nickel.

"I can understand that. How old is she?"

"Fifteen," Clint said, then smiled and added, "almost sixteen."

"So the partner is watching her?"

Again, Clint didn't reply.

"Okay, then," the lieutenant said. "Let me go to the chief's office and see if he's available. I'll be right back."

"I appreciate it."

After Abernathy left, Clint knew he was going to have to do some checking on the man before he fully believed that he was being frank. It could all be an act. Clint was sorry he could not take the man at face value, but he was just too cynical at this time in his life to do that.

And then there was the question of who in this department was in Cameron's pocket—like, for instance, the desk sergeant. Clint was going to have to assume that just as word had gone out to Cameron that he had checked into the hotel, word would get to him about his visit to the police department. Hell, he'd made sure of that himself with the desk clerk.

He was jolted from his reverie when the lieutenant returned.

"The chief will see you," he said. "This way."

Clint followed the lieutenant down a hall and was grateful that he was going to be able to judge the chief on his own, without hearing any baised opinions first.

TWENTY

While Clint was meeting with the chief of police, another meeting was taking place in a small, out-of-the-way hotel.

It was an odd thing how Franklin Walters's phobia about germs seemed to fly out the window when he was naked in bed with Olivia Cameron. At the moment his face was buried deep in her crotch. She had her long, slender legs spread as wide as she could, actually holding onto her ankles while the man worked on her with his tongue. He still didn't have the hang of this oral thing, and he wasn't any good at Frenching, but she was hoping to be able to whip him into shape sooner or later. She did not have any other suitable candidates for lovers, so she would have to make due with Walters.

She arched her back and released one ankle so she could stroke her own breast and pinch the nipple in the hopes of getting herself closer to orgasm.

Walters had seemed a good prospect because he was willing to fuck her in spite of the fact that she feared Louis Cameron. However, she soon learned his willingness was due more to her own attractiveness than any display of courage on his part. Simply put, he was unable to resist her—and that was before he was given a sample of her wares. Once he got a taste of Olivia, he was hooked.

"Easy, darling," she said, reaching down for his head, "right there . . . yes . . ."

Of course, she would have loved to find an experienced lover in Kansas City, one she could enjoy without it getting back to her husband. What Franklin Walters didn't know was that he had been approved by her husband, who probably assumed the man was woefully inept in bed and would pose no danger. He wasn't far from wrong.

"All right, Frankie," she said, sighing because her orgasm had managed to elude her, "time to poke it in Mommy's pussy."

Walters always assumed this was her term of endearment, calling herself Mommy, but she only ever did that when he frustrated her.

He mounted her and drove his rigid penis inside. He was able to get nice and hard, but she would have preferred a larger man—taller, more solid, with a longer dick. Ah well . . . she closed her eyes and moved her hips and pictured the huge, brutish sailor she had once picked up in a Barbary Coast saloon. That man had also been inept. All he'd wanted to do was poke it in her and then have a go—but my God, he was huge, filled her up with that big column of meat like no one before or since. If she'd only had time to work with him . . .

"Faster, darling," she told Walters, "and harder, oh, much harder, there's a good boy . . ."

When they were done, she watched him dress without interest. All she wanted at that moment was for him to leave. She was done with him. Once he was gone, she was going to have to bring herself to orgasm.

"Did you manage to find Joe Bravo?" she asked.

"Yes," he said, "he'll be in your husband's office at eleven."

"He's a gunman, isn't he?"

"Yes," Walters said, putting on his tie. "A young and very good gunman."

"Young?"

"Well, early thirties . . ."

"Like you?"

"Yes, like me."

In many ways Walter was a very mature thirty-one, but not in bed. But he was a good assistant for Louis, she knew.

"Is Louis going to send him after the Gunsmith?" she asked.

"I'm sure he is."

"That's a shame."

"Why?"

"Oh . . . just thinking out loud, darling. Be sure to pull the door shut on your way out."

He finished dressing and then went out the door without trying to kiss her. He'd learned the hard way she didn't like that. Just finish and get out.

Olivia had heard a lot of things about the Gunsmith over the years. In San Francisco, she'd talked with a couple of saloon girls who had been to bed with him. That was the reputation she was interested in, not his prowess with a gun.

Sliding her hands down between her legs, stroking herself, she wondered if she could manage to bed him before her husband managed to kill him.

TWENTY-ONE

Chief Dan Fortune was a large, broad-shouldered man in his fifties. He stood as Lieutenant Abernathy brought Clint into his office and extended his hand.

"Mr. Adams, it's a pleasure," Fortune said. "I'm acquainted with your reputation."

"It's something I have to carry around with me," Clint admitted.

"I don't mean your public reputation," Fortune said. "I mean what I've heard from people who know you."

"Such as?"

"Why don't you have a seat?" Fortune said. "Edgar, thank you."

Obviously, a dismissal. Lieutenant Abernathy nodded and left, closing the door behind him. The chief's office was four times the size of the lieutenant's, which made it about normal size. Apparently, the chief didn't feel the need for ostentation.

"We have friends in common," the chief said, taking his own seat

"Is that a fact?"

"I met Talbot Roper when he was in San Francisco on

a case," Fortune said. "I was a lieutenant then, like Abernathy. We worked together. He's a helluva detective."

"Yes, he is."

"I also know Duke Farrell."

Farrell ran a gambling house just off Portsmouth Square.

"I haven't seen Duke in years."

"I saw him several months ago, before I came here to take this job," Fortune said. "He said if I should run into you out here to give you his regards."

Clint made a mental note to telegraph both men—Roper and Farrell—for information about Fortune.

"Feel free to check me out with them," the man said, as if reading his mind.

"I will, thanks."

"Now," Fortune said, "the lieutenant didn't tell me what your business was, so why don't you tell me what I can do for you?"

"I came to Kansas City because I heard a friend of mine was murdered here," Clint explained.

"Oh?" Fortune looked concerned. "Who would that be?"

"Her name was Anne Archer," Clint said, then hurried on before the chief could speak. "I heard she was involved with William Cameron. I was wondering how the investigation is progressing."

"And did the lieutenant answer your question?"

"All he said was that he is still investigating," Clint answered, not wanting to get the lieutenant in trouble with his chief. "I think he brought me to you for more . . . in-depth answers."

"I'm afraid I don't have much to say to you that would be in-depth, Mr. Adams," Fortune said. "We are continuing to investigate."

"What about the connection to the Cameron family?"

"That is being looked into," Fortune said. "But you'll appreciate that something like that would have to be done . . . delicately."

"You mean because of the family's standing in the community?"

Instead of answering, Fortune stared at Clint for a few moments.

"All right, yes," he said, finally. "I could tell you that, but you're smart enough to know that it's more than that."

"Louis Cameron is a powerful man," Clint said, "and you have a job to be concerned about."

"I have a job to do," Fortune corrected him, "and a man like Cameron could make it much harder for me."

Clint spread his hands and said, "I understand. My only concern is that the whole thing is not swept under the rug."

"I'm not in the habit of having murders swept under the rug, Mr. Adams," Fortune bristled. "I don't care who's involved."

"I see," Clint said, standing. "Well, I guess I have my answer, then."

"Wait, wait," Fortune said, as Clint turned to leave. "What does that mean? What is your . . . interpretation of what just happened here?"

"My interpretation is that I'm going to have to look into the matter myself, Chief."

"You have no standing, Mr. Adams," the chief said. "I don't care who you are. I'll throw you in a cell if you start any trouble."

"I only intend to start trouble for one person, Chief."

"And who would that be?"

"Whoever was responsible for Anne Archer's death."

TWENTY-TWO

Franklin Walters—fresh from his second bath of the day—admitted Joe Bravo into Louis Cameron's office at eleven A.M. sharp.

"You smell sweet as a whore, Franklin," Bravo said to him as he went by.

Walters ignored him.

"You can close the door, Walters," Cameron said.

Walters withdrew from the room and did just that. He knew he smelled fresh, but Olivia must never know that he always went from her bed to a bath. She would feel insulted. He found it impossible to resist the woman, but after they were done he always felt dirty—full of germs—and had to run home to a fresh bath. She'd never understand that.

"He sure does smell good, don't he?" Bravo asked Cameron.

"Never mind that," Cameron said. "You mention it one more time and I'm going to think you're a nancy boy."

"Hey," Bravo said, "I like women all the way, old man."

"Joseph," Cameron said, "do you like my money?"

"I love it," Bravo said with a broad smile.

"Then don't ever let me hear you call me old man again."

"Uh, sure, Mr. Cameron," Bravo said. "Sorry."

"Have a seat," Cameron said. "We're going to talk about someone I'd like you to kill."

"Killin' is what I do best," Bravo said, having a seat. "Who did you have in mind?"

"How does the name Clint Adams sit with you?" Cameron asked.

Joe Bravo sat up straight and for once he did not have a silly grin on his face. Louis Cameron had never seen him look so serious.

"Is this on the level? The Gunsmith?"

"It's on the level, all right."

"Well, where do I find him?" Bravo asked. "I'll get it over with today."

"You're that confident?" Cameron asked.

"You better believe I'm confident, Mr. Cameron," he said. "Ain't a man alive can stand against me with a gun and live."

"If that's the case," Cameron said, "then you won't mind if I pay you after the deed is done?"

"You can pay me whenever you want, as long as I get my chance against the Gunsmith. You know what this will mean to my reputation?"

"Yes, I do, Joseph," Cameron said. "It means men will be coming after you the way they come after the Gunsmith."

"And they'll all be endin' up dead," Bravo said, "but first . . ."

"Yes, first," Cameron said. "You'll find that Adams is

staying at the Kansas City Plaza hotel. And I believe he's drinking at the Red Garter, across the street."

"I like the Red Garter," Bravo said. "That'd be a good place for people to watch me take down the Gunsmith."

"This has to be done fair and square," Cameron said, "or complete from ambush. There must be no questions either way."

"Oh, hell," Bravo said, "I got way too much respect for the Gunsmith to ambush him. No, this fella deserves to see it comin'."

"However you want to do it," Cameron said, "there will be two thousand dollars waiting here for you when you get back."

"You have that money ready today, Mr. Cameron," Bravo said, "because I ain't gonna waste no time with this."

"Oh, the money will be ready," Cameron assured him. "You just get the job done."

"You can bet on it."

Bravo got up and almost ran out the door, leaving it open behind him. Franklin Walters came walking in and closed it.

"What do you think, sir?" he asked. "Will he get the job done?"

"Why don't you get ahold of Denver Cole for me, Franklin. Get him here as fast as you can."

"Cole?" Walter asked. Denver Cole was a gunman of Clint Adams's generation, not Joe Bravo's. "Don't you think—"

"I think Clint Adams is going to kill that young fool and save me two thousand dollars."

TWENTY-THREE

Clint went directly from the police station to the nearest telegraph office. He sent three telegrams. First to his friend and most reliable source of information, Rick Hartman, in Labyrinth, Texas. From his table at Rick's Place, the saloon he owned, Rick could come up with more information than anyone Clint knew.

The second went to Talbot Roper, in Denver. Roper was the best private detective in the country and his opinion of Chief Fortune would mean a lot.

Third and last he sent a message to Duke Farrell. He hadn't been in touch with Farrell in years, but he knew the man would get back to him as soon as possible.

With that done, he collected Eclipse from the hotel livery. Apparently, the liveryman had had no trouble with the gelding the day before. Surprisingly, the man had managed to unsaddle Eclipse, then groom and feed him without getting kicked in the head.

"That's a fine animal," the liveryman told Clint. "High-spirited. Almost took a piece out of me, but then we came to an understanding."

"You didn't—" Clint started.

"I'd never harm an animal, mister, if that's what yer gonna ask," the man said. "I'm sayin' we had a talk and now we understand each other, don't we, boy?"

He put his hand on Eclipse's flank briefly and then removed it.

"He allows just the smallest touch, unless I'm groomin' him," the man said. "You bring 'im back and I'll do just that."

"We're just going for a short ride," Clint said. "We'll be back. What's your name?"

"Nate," the man said. "Folks around here just call me Nate."

"Okay, Nate, thanks." Clint walked Eclipse outside, then mounted him and rode over to Anne Archer's house.

"Father!" Sandy shouted when he entered. The word sounded strange to Clint, but also brought a lump to his throat.

He embraced the girl under the watchful eye of both her "aunts."

"Have you found Mother's killer?" she asked.

"Not yet," Clint said, "but I'm working on it."

"Do you want some coffee? I'll get it for you."

"Yes, I would like some." He touched her face. "Thank you."

She hurried to the kitchen, leaving him alone with Sandy and Katy.

"Did Sandy tell you what we talked about last night?" he asked Katy.

"You want us to go into hiding, Clint," Katy said. "That rubs me the wrong way."

"I figured it would, but Cameron's got so much money he could send an army against you."

"Or you."

"I can take care of myself, but not if I have to worry about—"

"We can take care of ourselves!" Katy said, cutting him off.

"—her," he finished, jerking his head toward the kitchen.

"Oh," Katy said. "Sorry."

"I need for the two of you to keep her safe while I finish this."

"We usually like to finish what we start ourselves, Clint," Sandy said. "And you need somebody to watch your back."

"Sandy—"

"Just hear me out before you complain," Sandy said, holding her hands up. "Before you came in, Katy and I came up with an answer."

"Which is?"

"One of us will take Sandy someplace safe," she said. "The other will stay to help you." She looked at Katy, who nodded her head in agreement.

"And were you able to decide which of you will do what?" he asked.

"We're still discussing that," Sandy admitted, a bit sheepishly.

"She means we're still arguing over that point," Katy commented.

"All right, then," he said. "That sounds like a plan to me—but get that last part cleared up quickly, like sometime today, huh?"

"We'll do that," Sandy promised.

"Can you tell us what you've been up to this morning?" Katy asked.

"How about over coffee?" Clint asked.

TWENTY-FOUR

After Clint finished the story about his visit with the police, Sandy said, "I have to admit, you've gotten more done in one morning than me and Katy have since Annie was killed."

"Sandy—" Katy said, with a warning look at Little Sandy.

"It's all right, Aunt Katy," the young Sandy said, "I know my mother was killed."

"I know you do, sweetie," Katy said, putting her hand over Sandy's. "I just . . . it's hard for me to realize that you're grown up."

"Grown up or not," Clint said, "somebody has to watch out for her." He stood up and regarded the two aunts. "You two make up your minds about who's staying and who's going. I'll come back this afternoon and we'll decide on a location."

"Location for what?" Little Sandy asked. "What's he talking about? Who's going where?"

"Your aunts will explain it to you, Sandy," Clint said. "I'll be back later."

"Where are you off to?" Katy asked.

"I told you I sent three telegrams," he said. "The men I sent them to will send me replies as soon as they get them. I'm going to check on that. I need to know if I can trust one of these policemen, or both, or neither."

"And if it's neither?" Sandy Spillane asked.

"Then we're on our own," Clint said.

Clint went to the telegraph office to check on his replies. He'd instructed the clerk not to send the replies to his hotel. He didn't want the clerk reading them and sending them to Louis G. Cameron. Then again, how did he know the telegraph clerk hadn't done that already? Well, it was a chance he'd already taken.

"Ah, your third reply just came in, sir," the clerk said happily. "Here they all are."

"Thank you."

Clint left the telegraph office and decided to read the replies over an early beer at the Red Garter.

When he entered, he saw that several other men had had the same idea for an early drink. They were scattered among the tables, with two at the bar.

He went to the bar and found Roscoe there, wiping glasses with a rag.

"Early start today, eh?" the bartender asked.

"Just a beer, Roscoe," Clint said.

"Comin' up."

Clint paid for the frosty mug and took it to a back table with him. He sat, sipped his beer and opened the first telegram.

It was from Rick Hartman. It said: *Know Fortune by reputation. Supposedly a straight shooter. Do not know Abnernathy.*

If Rick didn't know Abernathy, who would?

The second telegram was from Talbot Roper: *"Aber-nathy? From New Orleans? Beware. Good detective, but a loose cannon. Might be good fit for you. Fortune? Straight when he wants to be."*

The third was from Duke Farrell. It was brief: *"For-tune can't be bought."*

He sat back with his beer and wondered if he had learned anything he could use. None of the telegrams had been glowing in praise, nor particularly damning. It was useful to know that Fortune could not be bought, because that would be Cameron's stock-in-trade, buying people.

Clint knew there were six men in the saloon when he entered, and he had categorized them all before he even sat down. He wrote five of them off as no danger, but the sixth was a young man standing at the bar, nursing a beer and constantly wiping his palms dry on his pants. He was nervous and not without reason. He considered getting up and leaving, but thought that might push the boy into ac-tion. Maybe if he left the kid alone, he'd end up talking himself out of it.

He folded the three telegrams and put them in his pocket. Both men—Fortune and Abernathy—had earned themselves recommendations and warnings. That meant Clint was going to have to make his own decision about each of them.

The young man finally made his decision. He pushed away from the bar, wiped his gun hand off one more time on his thigh and then marched over to Clint's table.

"You Clint Adams?"

Clint looked up at him. Not shaving yet, but probably twenty-three. Another Billy the Kid wannabe.

"Who wants to know?"

"My name's Bravo, Joe Bravo."

Clint shrugged and shook his head.

"Doesn't mean anything to me."

"It will."

"That so?"

"When I kill you."

Clint chuckled.

"Kid, if you manage to kill me your name's not going to mean a thing to me."

Roscoe and the other men became aware of what was going on. They all stopped to watch.

"You got yourself an audience, kid," Clint said. "You sure you want them to see this?"

"All they're gonna see is me kill the Gunsmith," Bravo said.

"That so?"

"It is."

"You confident?"

"I am."

"I don't think you are," Clint said. "You keep wiping your hand on your thigh. I think if you drew your gun now it would slip right out of your sweaty hand. Why don't you go back to the bar, have another beer on me and think about it?"

Bravo wavered for a moment, then licked his lips and said, "I can't. I been waitin' for this for a long time."

"A long time? Kid, you haven't been alive for a long time."

"You gonna keep talkin'?" Bravo demanded. "I'll kill you where ya sit if you don't get up."

"You're going to have to do that, then," Clint said, "because I'm not standing up. Not for you."

Bravo frowned, unsure of what to do next.

"Whataya mean?"

"I mean I would stand up for a man who's earned my respect," Clint said. "You haven't done that."

"You know," Bravo snapped, "I was told I could bushwhack you but I wanted to give you the respect of facin' ya."

Clint frowned.

"Bushwhack me? Son, somebody put you up to this?" Clint asked.

Bravo backed off, seemed to realize he'd said too much.

"I don't need nobody to put me up to this," he said. "I told you I been waitin' for this. Now stand up or I'll plug ya where ya sit!"

"Roscoe, you know this kid?"

"He's been around here a while," Roscoe said, leaning on the bar.

"Is he serious?"

"He is."

"Then I'm going to have to kill him."

"Afraid so."

"Stop talkin' about me like I'm not here!"

"Last time, kid," Clint said. "Take a walk."

"I'm not leavin'."

"Then do something."

Clint sat there, slouched, seemingly relaxed, staring up at the younger man.

"Damn you!" Bravo shouted, and went for his gun. As he did so, Clint kicked the chair opposite him into Bravo, knocking him of balance. Clint came out of his chair, closed the distance between the two of them and snatched the gun from Bravo's hand. Then he pushed the young man, sending him spinning and sprawling into the center of the room.

Clint closed on him again, got down on one knee and asked, "Tell me who put you up to this?"

"Whataya doin'?"

"Keeping you alive," Clint said, then pointed the young man's own gun at him, cocked the hammer and added, "Maybe."

Bravo stared down the barrel of his own gun and asked, "W-whataya wanna know?"

TWENTY-FIVE

When Clint got back to his hotel, Lieutenant Abernathy was waiting in the lobby.

"Waiting long?" Clint asked.

"Long enough," the man said. "We need to talk, away from the police station."

"And away from here," Clint said, sliding a glance toward the clerk, hoping that Abernathy understood.

"I know a place," the policeman said. "Come with me."

They left the hotel.

"You know a kid named Joe Bravo?" Clint asked as they walked.

"Would-be gunman," Abernathy said. "Hasn't killed anybody yet, as far as I know, but he's supposed to be pretty good with his gun."

"He tried to kill me."

"When?"

"About twenty minutes ago."

"What happened?"

"I took his gun away from him and kicked him out of town."

"Was he just trying to make a name for himself?"

"He says he was hired by Louis Cameron."

Abernathy stopped.

"What?"

"That's what he said."

"And you let him leave town?"

"I don't want Cameron for hiring some kid to kill me. I want him for Anne Archer's murder."

They started walking again.

"Well, you must be worrying him."

"Not if he sent a kid like Joe Bravo," Clint said. "I think maybe he just wanted to see what I would do."

"You're thinking he sent the kid because who'd believe him when he said he was hired?"

"Right. Why would someone with Cameron's money and influence hire a child? If and when he wants me dead, he'll hire somebody who can do the job."

"Is there somebody?"

"What do you mean?"

"That can do the job?" Lieutenant Abernathy asked. "Kill you?"

"Anybody can shoot a bullet in my back," Clint said. "Are you asking me if there's someone out there who can outdraw me? Kill me in a fair fight?"

"Yes," the man said, "that's what I'm asking."

"I'm sure there is," Clint said. "Thankfully, I've never met him, and I hope I don't anytime soon."

Walters entered his boss's office quietly. It wasn't so he wouldn't disturb him at work. It was so he wouldn't wake him. The old man had dozed off in his chair.

He approached the desk slowly, realizing that he could put a bullet in the old man's head right then and there.

Olivia would get half of his money—with the other half going to Billy—and he, Walters, would get Olivia.

Even if he'd had a gun, though, he couldn't have done it. He wasn't a killer. He'd told that to Olivia more than once.

Abruptly, the old man opened his eyes, and Walters wondered if he was playing possum.

"What is it, Walters? Is Bravo dead?"

"No, sir, but neither is Adams," Walters said. "I got word that Adams disarmed the boy and sent him scampering out of town."

"Did he tell Adams I hired him?"

"Right in the middle of the Red Garter."

"How many people heard?"

"Not many," Walters said. "It was mostly empty at the time."

"No one would believe him, anyway," Cameron said. "So, Adams is not the trigger-happy killer his reputation makes him out to be."

"Apparently not."

"Good," the old man said. "Then maybe he's not as good as everybody says he is."

"Maybe Denver Cole will find that out for you, sir," Walters said.

"Have you heard from him?"

"Yes, sir, he'll be here tomorrow."

"Excellent. Have you seen Billy today?"

"No, sir."

"What the hell is that boy up to?" the old man wondered aloud.

"He's still pretty upset."

"About the Archer woman?" Cameron waved that off. "He'll get over it."

"Yes, sir."

"All right, Walters, that's all."

"Yes, sir."

"Just locate my son and tell him I want to see him—today!"

"I'll get right on it, sir."

"And Walters."

"Sir?"

"Have you seen Mrs. Cameron today?"

"I haven't," Walters lied. "No, sir." '

Cameron smiled and said, "That's all."

TWENTY-SIX

Abernathy took Clint to a small saloon about two blocks off the main street where he didn't think anyone would see them together.

"And if they do," he explained, "I'll just say I was questioning you."

They got a beer each from the silent bartender and took them to a back table.

"I understand you usually sit with your back to the wall," the policeman said.

"It's preferable," Clint said, "except when I'm with someone I trust to watch my back."

Clint took the chair against the wall.

"If Louis Cameron sent Joe Bravo to kill you," Abernathy said, "or to test you, then it seems fairly certain that he had your friend killed."

"Or maybe his son killed her and he's covering for him."

"That's a possibility," Abernathy said, "but by all accounts I've heard, Billy was in love with Miss Archer."

"And did his wife know that?"

"If I heard it, I'm sure she heard it, too."

"Then she could've had Anne killed."

Abernathy spread his hands.

"You see? All my suspects come from that family, but they are untouchable."

"By whose order?"

"By the mere fact that they are the Cameron family," the lieutenant said. "Louis Cameron is the most powerful man in the state, Mr. Adams. As much as I, or my chief, would like to solve this case, there are people who won't allow it."

"Legally."

"Yes," Abernathy agreed, "legally."

"And that's why you're here with me," Clint said. "Because I can do things you can't."

"Mr. Adams," Abernathy said, "Cameron is a rich and powerful man, but in your own way you are Old West royalty. Do you know what I mean?"

"Yes, I'm afraid I do."

Abernathy told him anyway.

"The stories of the Gunsmith, of Billy the Kid, of Jesse James—"

"You're lumping me in with a bunch of dead men," Clint pointed out.

"Very well then—Wyatt Earp, Bat Masterson, Bill Tilghman—you have all been immortalized in dime novels written by Ned Buntline and his kind."

"That makes us legends back East," Clint said, "where people know nothing of what it takes to live out here. Where they all believe what they read."

"Don't be so quick to dismiss your standing here in the West, Mr. Adams," the man said. "Even out here you are held in high regard."

"Yeah, so high that every punk with a gun wants to take a shot at immortality."

"But we are discussing what you may be able to do here in Kansas City," Abernathy said, "perhaps making use of your reputation."

"So what you're saying," Clint said, "is that Louis Cameron and Clint Adams are above the law."

"That is not something I would ever say too loud," Abernathy said, "but in this instance I'm afraid it might apply."

"So are you saying that if I find out that Cameron had Anne killed, and I kill him . . . I'll get away with it?"

Abernathy regarded Clint above the rim of his beer mug and said, "I would never say that . . . very loud."

Billy Cameron lifted his head from the table and stared up at Franklin Walters.

"Hello, Wally."

He was the only person who called Walters "Wally."

"Billy, your father wants to see you," Walters said. "We have to get you clean and sober."

"Wally, Wally, Wally," Cameron said, "my buddy."

He tried to put his head back down in the puddle of beer he'd been sleeping in, but Walters stopped him. With his hand wrapped in a white handkerchief he grabbed Billy by the elbow and pulled.

"Up, Billy," he said. "Come on, I'm going to take you home and you're going to sober up."

"Why?" Billy asked, staring at Walters myopically. "I'm just gon' get drunk again."

"You're free to do that," Walters said, "after you talk to your father."

"Aw, what's he want?" Billy demanded as Walters steered him to the door of the little saloon.

"I don't know," Walters said. "I suppose when you get there you'll have to ask him."

Outside, Cameron asked, "Why you doin' this, Wally? 'Cuz you like me?"

"Because it's my job, Billy," Walters said. "Because it's my job."

TWENTY-SEVEN

Clint and Abernathy left the small side street saloon and stopped right outside.

"Chief Fortune send you to me, Lieutenant?" Clint asked.

"The chief does not know I am talking to you," Abernathy said.

"When you said today that they put you in that closet office to try to get you to quit, were you talking about him?"

"I was just talking," Abernathy said. "Complaining. Don't all civil servants complain about their jobs, their salaries?"

"All the ones I've known have."

"Well, there you go . . ."

"Do you still want me to come to you with what I find out?" Clint asked. "Or shall I just . . . act on it?"

"I am conducting an active investigation, Mr. Adams," Abernathy said officially. "I expect you to come to me with anything that you find out."

"Fair enough," Clint said.

• • •

When Franklin Walters walked Billy Cameron into his father's office, he was far from sober. Walters guided Billy to a chair and into it, then looked at his boss.

"That's fine, Walters," Cameron said, waving. "You can go."

"Yes, sir."

As Walters closed the door, the old man stared at his son in disgust.

"What are you doing to yourself, Billy?"

He was wearing fresh clothing and had washed up, but there was still whiskey leaking from his pores.

"Whataya think, Pop?"

"You're trying to kill yourself?" Cameron asked. "Over that woman? Is that it?"

"You made me marry Lorna, pop," Billy Cameron said. "I never loved her."

"I know that, and so does she," Cameron said. "It made good sense, is all. But that . . . woman?"

"Be careful what you say about her—"

"Fine, fine," Cameron said. "Get drunk if you want to—stay drunk, too, but do it at home, huh? Don't do it in public."

"Yeah, yeah," Billy said, "I wouldn't want to embarrass the family."

"No, you wouldn't," Cameron said. "Just remember that. Now go home, crawl into a bottle. Get it out of your system."

Billy got to his feet, stumbled, regained his balance and made his way to the door. Cameron watched, both disgusted and dismayed. This was the man who was going to take over the empire. He was going to have to talk to Lorna. The woman was lovely. Surely, she could use her considerable talents to make her husband forget the dead woman.

Clint had decided to make a bold move after leaving Lieutenant Abernathy. Why not beard the lion in his own den?

He entered Louis G. Cameron's office, located in another of Kansas City's more modern brick structures. The slender man seated at the desk looked up and frowned.

"Mr. Cameron sees no one without an appointment," he said.

"How do you know I don't have an appointment?" Clint asked.

The man smiled.

"Because I make all his appointments."

At that point the door to Cameron's office opened and a young man came staggering out. He almost bumped into Clint and kept going out the door.

"Did he have an appointment?"

"That was Mr. Cameron's son."

"Ah," Clint said, "the famous Billy I've been hearing so much about."

"And who would you be?"

"You first," Clint said.

"I am Franklin Walters, Mr. Cameron's assistant," the man said.

"Well, my name is Clint Adams," Clint said. "I think Mr. Cameron will see me . . . don't you?"

The man stared at Clint with his mouth open, then got up and said, "I-I'll see."

"You do that."

He stumbled to the office door and through it in a good impersonation of drunk Billy Cameron. As Clint waited, he sniffed the air. The whiskey smell coming off of Billy was still there. He had a feeling father and son were not getting along well.

"What is it, Walters?" Cameron asked, annoyed. "Billy staggers out and now you come stumbling in?"

"Um, Clint Adams is outside to see you."

"What? Are you sure it's him?"

"Well, he said he wa—"

"Never mind," Cameron said. He opened the top drawer of his desk, took out a gun, checked to make sure it was loaded, then replaced it. He left the drawer ajar. "All right, show him in."

"Are you sure—"

"Oh, show him in, Walters!"

"Yes, sir."

Clint waited patiently until the door finally opened and the assistant came out.

"You can go in, sir."

"Why, thank you, Walters," Clint said, moving past the man.

He closed the door firmly in Walter's face.

"Mr. Cameron?" he asked the old man behind the desk.

"I'm Cameron," the man said in a raspy voice. "You're supposed to be Clint Adams?"

"I am," Clint said. "I'm the man you sent a boy named Joe Bravo to kill."

"I did nothing of the kind," Cameron said. "I have no idea what you're talking about."

Clint approached the desk, noticed the man's right hand twitch near a partially open desk drawer.

"I doubt that very much, Mr. Cameron," Clint said.

"From what I've heard about you, you always know what's going on."

"That may be, but you're talking crazy," Cameron said. "Why would I send a boy to kill you?"

"You're right," Clint said. "You wouldn't. You sent him to test me. When you do send someone to kill me, it'll be a man, won't it?"

"Still taking crazy, sir."

"That was your son leaving here, wasn't it?" Clint asked. "Actually, I need to talk to him as well."

"I would stay away from my son if I were you, sir," Cameron said warningly.

"Is that right? Why's that? You and he have a fight? Are you afraid of what he might say?"

He could tell Louis Cameron did not like being braced in his own office. His right hand was twitching. He had a feeling if the old man had been just a few years younger he would have gone for that gun in the drawer.

"You want to grab that gun in your drawer, I'll give you a head start, old man," Clint said.

Cameron pulled his hand back as if he had been suddenly burned.

"Good choice," Clint said. "Live a little longer."

"I'm not sure you have anything to say to me, Mr. Adams, so get out of my office."

"Let me make this clear before I leave," Clint said. "I know you had something to do with the death of Anne Archer. I'm going to find out who pulled the trigger on her, and after I take care of that I'll trace the killer back to you. And then I'll be back and we'll see if you have the nerve to go for that gun in the drawer."

Cameron glared at him with hatred.

"I'm going to turn my back now and walk out," Clint

said. "You'll have a chance to try to shoot me in the back."

Clint turned, walked to the door, then looked around and stared hard at Cameron, who hadn't moved.

"Good choice."

TWENTY-EIGHT

While Clint Adams was in with Louis Cameron, Olivia Cameron entered the outer office.

"Is he in?" she asked Walters. "What am I saying? Of course he's in. Where else would he be, darling?"

"Don't call me that here," Walters hissed. "He's inside with Clint Adams."

"Clint Adams?" she asked. "Really?" She had only ever heard of the man, but she was thrilled.

Suddenly, the door opened and a tall man stepped out.

"Hey, Walters," Clint said, "better get your boss some water. I think his mouth's a little dry."

"What did you do—"

"Mr. Adams?"

Clint turned and saw an absolutely lovely woman standing there with a blue dress that hugged every curve of her.

"Yes?"

"I just—well, it's just a pleasure to meet you, sir," she said. "My name is Olivia Cameron. The man with the dry mouth is my husband."

"Really?" Clint asked. "You and him?"

Walters wanted to stay and listen to their conversation, but he also felt he should go into the office and check on his boss.

"I know," she said, "it's hard to believe, but . . ." She shrugged.

"Mrs. Cameron—"

"Oh, Olivia, please."

"Olivia," he said, "I was just going to go try to find a good cup of coffee and a piece of peach pie. Would you be able to recommend someplace?"

"Why, yes, there's a perfectly nice—"

"And would you join me?"

Her eyes widened and her breathing deepened, which did nice things to her chest.

"I would love to join you."

"Well, then let's go," he said, extending his arm.

She slid her arm into his and they left right away. Walters came rushing out of the office just in time to see them go. He opened his mouth to protest, but then shut it quickly.

After all, what could he have said?

"What was your business with my husband?" Olivia asked when they got outside.

"Why should we talk about that?" he asked. "Which way to the peach pie?"

She giggled and said, "This way," tugging on his arm.

Walters didn't know what to do so he went back into the office, where Cameron had just kicked him out.

"What the hell do you want?" the old man demanded. He was holding a tumbler of whiskey and his hand was shaking. "I told you I don't want any damn water."

"I . . . Olivia just walked in the door, and—"

"I don't want to see her."

"Uh, no, I mean . . . she left."

"So?"

"With him."

"With who?"

"With the Gunsmith."

"You're telling me my wife just left with Clint Adams?"

"Yes, sir."

"And you let her go?"

"H-how could I have stopped them?"

Cameron stared at Walters for a moment, then said, "How, indeed. Walters, come have a glass of whiskey."

"Yes, sir!"

TWENTY-NINE

"You strike me as being a smart woman," Clint told Olivia when they were seated with coffee and pie in front of them.

"Really?" she asked. "Little ol' me?"

"I think a lot of men buy into your act," he went on, "like your husband."

She sat back and lowered her voice about an octave.

"Oh, you can bet he bought it," she said. "But you know what? He's no dope. He bought what he wanted, and I give it to him."

"And what did he want?"

"A beautiful wife to wear on his arm."

"And that's it?"

"You mean, do I share his bed?" She shuddered. "No, we have a strict hands-off policy."

"So what do you do when you want . . . hands on?"

She smiled.

"I pick the hands I want on me," she said, "but so far I've had nothing but disappointment in Kansas City. There seems to be no men here who know what to do with a woman."

"That's a shame," he said. "A woman like you deserves to be handled right."

"You know," she said, leaning forward and giving him the full effect of her green eyes, "I've heard stories about you."

"You can't believe everything you hear," he said. "Nobody alive can have killed as many men as I'm given credit for."

"Oh," she said, "I wasn't talking about your prowess with a gun."

"Oh?"

"Before I lived here," she said, "I lived in San Francisco. I met several women who had many . . . nice things to say about you."

"That's good to hear," Clint said. "I mean, having people say something nice about me for a change."

"Oh," she said, "they were very complimentary."

Clint leaned over his half-eaten pie and said, "And you're curious, aren't you?"

"To tell you the truth," she said, "I'm desperate, and you just may be the answer to a girl's prayer."

"So where do we go from here, Olivia?"

"I'll bet you have a room in the best hotel in town."

"You'd win that bet."

"Then I say we go there."

THIRTY

Clint thoroughly enjoyed escorting Olivia Cameron under the clerk's nose, because he knew word would get back to her husband.

When they got to his suite, she looked around and asked, "How did you rate the best suite in the house?"

"Maybe I scared the clerk," Clint said.

"You know my husband owns this hotel."

"I suspected as much," he said. "Word got back to your husband pretty quick that I checked in."

"Word gets back to my husband about everything."

"It doesn't bother you that he'll hear about this?"

"Oh, no," she said. "It will kill him, especially if you and he are doing business."

"We're not doing business, exactly," Clint said.

She began to loosen the stays on her dress and slip out of it.

"You see, I believe your husband had a friend of mine killed."

She stopped just for a second, then stepped out of the dress and said, "Oh, yes? You'll have to tell me about that . . . later."

She undid her undergarments, let them fall to the ground, and then stood with her hands on her hips.

"You see this?" she asked. "My husband is paying a lot of money for this—and he's not allowed to touch."

Clint eyed her firm breasts, slender waist, long legs and the bush between her legs and said, "A fool and his money . . ."

If Olivia Cameron was disappointed with Clint's performance, she was making too much noise to notice.

Clint shucked his clothes quickly and took the woman to bed, determined to make sure she had a time to remember. Also, he apparently had a reputation with the ladies in San Francisco to live up to.

Most of all he wondered if Olivia would go home and tell her husband all about her afternoon.

Normally, Clint would have turned her advance down. She was prideful, and she was married, two things he did not like in a woman. But even though he was doing this to get to her husband, there was no harm in enjoying a beautiful woman.

Holding her in bed, he realized she had quite a beautiful mouth. Her upper lip was almost as full as the lower, and when he kissed her it was a wonderful experience. She moaned deep in her throat, slid her hands down his body until she had hold of his erection.

"Oh, God, yes," she said, sliding her mouth from his, "I want to get a close look at you."

"Not yet," he whispered, "first I get to look at you . . . and touch you."

He kissed her neck, slid his hand over one breast, then the other before leaning down to kiss them. Her skin was pale and smooth, her nipples dark brown. He took one in his mouth, rolled it around with his tongue while he slid his hand down to her moist pussy. He used a finger to part the slick lips and then slid the tip of his finger up and down, making her moan and move her legs. He bit her nipple, then moved to the other one and spent some time there before moving his mouth down, working his way along her body. He tickled her belly button with the tip of his tongue, kissed her belly, moved down farther and nuzzled her pubic bush with his nose. The scent of her wetness was heady and he delved in with his tongue until he could taste her. Her body jerked and she cried out when the tip of his tongue found her clit. He slid his hands beneath her to cup her buttocks and lift her off the bed. This gave him a better angle to work on her pussy with his mouth and tongue until she was writhing on the bed, banging her fists on the mattress, tossing her head from side to side crying out, "That's it! That's it! That's what I've been missing . . ."

Moments later she was sitting on the bed with her knees pulled up to her chest, catching her breath.

"Finally," she said, "a man who knows how to touch a woman."

"I'm sorry you've had to wait so long," he said, sitting across from her.

"So am I," she said. "Jesus." She touched her left breast. "I thought I was going to have a heart attack. I mean, so much pleasure after waiting so long."

She stretched her legs out then, put her hands behind her and leaned back. This position thrusted her breasts out and he could see that her dark nipples were still hard. He could also still smell her. The scent of her excitement permeated the room.

"Now," she said, eyeing him up and down, "it's my turn . . ."

"Me?"

She quickly got to her knees, put her hands against his chest and pushed him over backward until he was lying on his back with his head at the foot of the bed.

She got down between his spread legs and took his hard dick in her hands. She licked the underside of it, stopping just beneath the head when he jerked. She began to suck just the head of his cock, while continuing to flick that sensitive spot with the tip of her tongue.

"You are the prettiest man . . ." she cooed. She slid one hand down to cup his testicles and then took the length of him inside her hot mouth. She held him there for several seconds, then began to bob her head up and down, suckling him wetly.

"Mmmm," she murmured, as her head began to move faster and faster. He reached down to put his hands on her head, but he exerted no pressure. His hands just rode with her and then he began to move his hips in unison.

Finally, she released him, slid on top of him and guided him inside her.

"Ooooh, yessss," she hissed as she sat down on him, taking him all the way in. She closed her eyes, said, "This is going to be good," and then started riding him.

She was right.

It was.

Later they were lying in bed together, knowing that it was time to get dressed and go their separate ways.

"You did this just to get to my husband, didn't you?" she asked.

"That was my initial thought, yes," he said, "but that doesn't mean I didn't enjoy it."

"Oh, I know you enjoyed it," she said, her eyes glittering. "So did I. You've ruined me now for the men in Kansas City."

"Then I feel bad for the men of Kansas City."

She sat up, pulled on her underthings and stood up to put her dress back on. Then she went to the mirror to try to do something with her hair.

"You know," she said, looking at his reflection, "he's a horrible, horrible man who will do anything to get what he wants."

"That's what I've heard."

"But he's been nothing but good to me."

"Then why do you . . ."

"What? Sleep with other men? Well, I do have needs," she said, then turned and said, "In my own way, I'm as selfish as he is."

"But not horrible."

"No," she said, "not horrible."

She walked to the bed, reached out and took his hand in both of hers.

"I wonder . . ."

"Yes?"

"Should you get what you want . . . do you think you can do that without . . . killing him?"

"Olivia," he said, "believe it or not, I'd prefer to do that. But I think that's going to be up to him."

She nodded, as if she understood, and he squeezed her hand.

"You know, he's very lucky to have someone like you to beg for his life."

"Well, I have another hope, too," she said, moving to the door.

"What's that?"

"I hope that if you don't get what you want," she said, "that he won't end up killing you."

As she went out the door, he said, "Believe it or not, I'd prefer that, too."

THIRTY-ONE

When Clint came down, he boldly looked over at the clerk, who averted his eyes. He wondered if that man had sent a message over to Cameron that his wife had been there with Clint Adams. Or was he too afraid to give the old man that kind of news?

Walking to the front door, Clint saw Sandy Spillane sitting in a wooden chair, her arms folded across her full breasts.

"I won," she said, looking up at him. "Katy took Little Sandy someplace safe."

"Good," he said, "then I don't have to worry about her anymore."

"I saw Olivia Cameron leave," Sandy said. "She looked a little . . . disheveled? Is that the word?"

"Sandy, I can explain—"

She stood up and said, "You don't have to explain anything to me, Clint. What you do with you time is your own business. As long as you don't forget what we're doin' here."

"I'm not forgetting anything," he said. "I went to see Cameron and his wife was—"

"You went to see him?" she asked, cutting him off. "Why?"

"I wanted him to know I know," he said. "I wanted him to know I'm coming for him."

"So you warned him that you were coming," she said. "Now he'll be ready."

"He had his chance," Clint said. "He had a gun in his desk and his hand was shaking too much to use it."

"And you think that was from fear?" she asked. "He's an old man, Clint, his hand always shakes."

"That may be . . ."

"So what are you going to do next?"

"Next I want to talk to the son, Billy," he said. "He was there, too, and he's pretty drunk. Looks like he's been drunk for a while."

"Well, supposedly he was really in love with Annie," Sandy said. She shrugged. "Who knows?"

"Where does he live?"

"I'll take you there," she said. "I can watch your back, and be your chaperone."

"Chaperone?"

"His wife is very beautiful, too, like Olivia."

THIRTY-TWO

Billy Cameron and his wife lived in a huge house in a section of the city that had plenty of them, but this one—looking like it had been plucked off a plantation in South Carolina—was the jewel of the lot.

"Jesus," Clint said, "where does the old man live?"

"Oh," Sandy said, "he's got a big house."

They approached the front door and Clint knocked firmly. He was about to knock again when the door was suddenly opened by a middle-aged black woman wearing a maid's uniform. Clint was surprised it wasn't a black man in a suit and white gloves.

"Yassuh?"

"I'm here to see Mr. Cameron, please."

"Mr. Cameron, he under the weathuh at the moment."

"I see. Well, what about Mrs. Cameron?"

"She here."

"Can I see her?"

"I'll check."

She closed the door.

"That reminds me," Clint said. "You know a black man named Leon, works at my hotel as a porter?"

"No, why? Should I?"

"Well, he warned me about the clerk carrying messages to Louis Cameron," Clint said, "and he doesn't really talk like an uneducated black man."

"What are you thinkin'?"

"Does Pinkerton have any black operatives that you know of?"

"One or two."

"Have you met them?"

"I've seen them."

"Well, then, maybe you should take a look at this fellow when we get finished here."

The door opened and the maid reappeared.

"Madam says she'll see you in the study."

"That's fine."

"Follow me, please."

Clint allowed Sandy to enter ahead of him, then went in and closed the door behind them. They followed the maid through the huge entry foyer to a hallway, and then along the hall to the study, where Mrs. Cameron was waiting.

Sandy had been right. The woman was beautiful. She was just a little younger than Olivia, with red hair and pale skin. She was long and lean, with beautiful green eyes. In fact, she had the same general coloring that Anne Archer had.

Odd.

"I assume you are Clint Adams?" the woman asked.

"That's right," Clint said. "How did you—"

"My father-in-law warned me that you might come here," she said. "He advised me not to see you."

"And yet you agreed."

"Yes," she said. "I rarely do as my father-in-law . . . orders."

She approached him and extended her hand.

"My name is Lorna Cameron."

"I'm happy to meet you," Clint said. "This is my colleague, Sandy Spillane."

"How do you do."

Lorna Cameron was definitely from the East, he could tell from her accent and her manner.

"You wanted to see Billy. He's not . . . feeling very well at the moment."

"I saw him at your father-in-law's office this morning," Clint said.

"Then you know he's drunk, not sick."

"Yes."

"He's been drunk for . . . quite some time."

"I think I know how long he's been drunk, Mrs. Cameron."

"Yes," she said, "since that . . . woman was killed."

"We think someone in your family is responsible for killing her, Mrs. Cameron," Sandy said.

"Yes, well, that wouldn't surprise me. My father-in-law is capable of anything."

"You think it was him?" Clint asked.

"Oh, he'd have someone else do it for him," she said. "He'd never get his own hands dirty."

"But why would he have her killed?"

"That's simple," she said. "She was corrupting his precious Billy."

"Couldn't that also be a motive for you, Mrs. Cameron?" Sandy asked.

Lorna Cameron looked at Sandy Spillane and lifted her chin up.

"I suppose it could," she said, "if I cared."

"And you don't?" Clint asked.

"I did," she said, "once, but that seems like a long time ago. I'm tired of being the only one who cares. The men in this family have turned me cold, I'm afraid."

Icy cold, Clint was thinking as he looked at her.

"Would you like to go upstairs and wake Billy up?" she asked. "I'm not sure you'll get very much out of him."

"No, that's all right," Clint said. "Tell him I was here, though."

"I will," she said. "I'll also tell my father-in-law, if that's all right with you."

"That's fine," Clint said. "Thank you for seeing us."

As Clint turned to leave, Sandy stepped up and asked, "Mrs. Cameron, do you think your husband could have killed Anne Archer?"

"I understand he was quite smitten with her," she said. "However, my husband has the Cameron temper. If she rejected him at one point, I wouldn't be surprised if he killed her."

"Thank you for being honest."

"Mr. Adams," she said, "I would watch my back if I were you. My father-in-law is almost certain to try to have you killed."

"Mrs. Cameron," Clint said, "I always watch my back. It's a way of life with me."

She apparently wasn't sure what to say to that. Clint and Sandy turned and left.

THIRTY-THREE

Clint and Sandy walked back to the Plaza because he wanted her to get a look at the black porter he'd told her about.

"Hey, where's Leon?" Clint asked the clerk as he entered.

"W-who?" the clerk asked nervously.

"Leon, the black porter who took my things to my room when I checked in. I want to give him a dollar tip."

"Um, Leon doesn't work here anymore," the clerk said.

"What are you talking about?" Clint asked.

"He, uh, had to leave all of a sudden," the man said.

Clint walked over to the desk to confront the man.

"Why?"

"I uh, don't know," the clerk stammered. "F-family emergency, I guess."

Clint looked at Sandy.

"This isn't right." He reached out, grabbed the front of the clerk's shirt and pulled the man halfway across the desk.

"Now you listen good, because I'm not going to ask you again," Clint said. "What happened to Leon?"

"I don't know, I swear," the clerk said. "All I know is Mr. Walters came in and told me I had to fire him."

"Do you know where Leon lives?"

"A small house, across the tracks," the clerk said. "You know, in the black section."

"What house?"

"I don't know!"

Clint released the man, pushed him so hard he banged into the key setup, knocking the entire thing over so that keys rang as they hit the floor.

He turned to Sandy and said, "We've got to find him. Something may have happened to him."

They started for the door, but Clint stopped, turned and pointed his finger at the clerk.

"If you send a message about this to Louis Cameron, I'll come back and put a bullet in your ear. I swear!"

"Yes, sir! No, sir!"

"Come on," he said to Sandy.

Outside, she said, "Wow, I really believed you would come back and shoot him."

"I will," Clint growled.

The section of the city where most of the blacks lived was quite a contrast to where Billy Cameron lived with his wife. The place was filled with run-down, if not falling down, shacks. There were woman outside doing laundry in tin basins, men just sitting outside smoking and drinking. Clint and Sandy drew looks—especially Sandy with her blond hair and full body.

Sandy wanted to start asking questions, but Clint waited until they came to one house where a man and a woman were outside with two small children before he asked, "Do you know where a man named Leon lives?"

"We gots lots of Leons," the man said. "What's his last name?"

"I don't know," Clint said, "but he works as a porter at the Plaza hotel."

"Whatchoo wan' wit' him?" the man asked suspiciously.

"I want to make sure he's still alive," Clint said.

"What make you t'ink he ain't?"

"Look," Clint said, "I know he's not from here, I know he wasn't really working at the hotel because he had to."

"You work for dat man Cameron?" the man asked.

"No, Leon did me a favor and warned me about Cameron. I just want to make sure he's okay."

The man studied Clint, then got up out of his chair. He walked over to where his son and daughter were playing, grabbed the boy—who was about eight—and whispered something into his ear. The boy nodded and took off running.

"You want some shine while you wait?" the man asked. "I got some good shine."

"No," Clint said, "thanks. We'll just wait."

"The lady can set," the man said, pointing to his chair.

"Thank you," Sandy said. She didn't want to sit, but didn't want to refuse the kindness.

"You ain't law," the man observed.

"No," Clint replied.

The man looked at Sandy.

"You ain't law."

"No."

The man nodded, satisfied that he had them figured right.

"What makes you think we're not law?" Sandy asked.

"If you was law, you wouldn't be askin'," the man said, "you'd be tellin'."

Clint thought that was a good way to note the difference.

THIRTY-FOUR

It only took fifteen minutes for the little boy to come back with Leon in tow.

"You know this feller, Leon?" the other man asked.

"Yes, I know him, Daniel. This is Mr. Clint Adams."

Daniel's eyebrows shot up. Since meeting him, Clint had been trying to guess his age. He could have been anywhere between thirty and sixty.

"Mr. Gunsmith himself?" Daniel asked.

"That's right," Leon said, "and this is Miss Sandy Spillane, late of the Pinkerton Agency."

"Clint," Sandy said, "this is Ken Leon, also from the Pinkerton Agency. Kenny, what the hell are you doing here?"

"Let's take a walk," Kenny Leon said. "Daniel, excuse us."

"Go ahead and have your secrets," Daniel said. "I ain't want no part o' them."

"Oh, Clint? Would you give young David here two bits? I promised him you would."

"Why don't you give it to him?"

"He'd rather have it from the Gunsmith."

Clint dug out two bits and flipped it to the boy, who caught it one-handed.

"Thank yuh, suh."

"Anytime, David."

"Now . . ." Leon said, taking both their elbows and leading them away while walking between them.

"First of all," he said to Sandy, "Mr. Pinkerton just thought you might need some backup."

"Because he didn't think a bunch of women could do the job?" Sandy demanded.

"Well, look at the way things have turned out, Sandy," Leon said. "Anne is dead."

"That means you weren't very good at your job of being backup, doesn't it, Leon?" Clint asked.

Leon looked at Clint, then looked away and said, "You got me there."

"Look, Leon," Sandy said, "we don't blame you for Annie's death—"

"No, no, that's okay," Leon said. "I think Mr. Pinkerton might be considering firing me because of it."

"What happened at the hotel?" Clint asked. "Why did you get fired?"

"Oh, some white woman accused the black porter of staring at her," he said. "At least, that's the story I got."

"What do you think happened?"

"Not sure," Leon said. "If they were suspicious of me, I probably would've ended up like Anne, so I don't know. All I know is I'm not in a position to do anybody any good."

"Well," Clint said, "we might need you if this goes to the street."

Leon stopped short and looked at Clint.

"You mean gunplay?" he shook his head. "I'm an operative, I'm not a gunman. I wouldn't be any damn good to you."

"If you can't handle a gun, Leon," Clint asked, "then how exactly were you going to back these ladies up, when they're the ones who can handle a gun?"

"Hey," Leon said, "I just did what I was told."

Clint realized that Leon was right. He was no good to them at all.

"Okay, Leon," Clint said, "I just wanted to make sure you didn't get killed for warning me."

"Well, I'm fine," he said, "and I can help if—"

"No, Leon," Clint said, "I'm going to take you at your word. You probably are no damn good to us right now."

THIRTY-FIVE

Clint and Sandy had supper together in a café she knew. They both ordered steak platters and big glasses of cold beer.

"Where are you staying?" he asked her. "Still at the house?"

"Might as well," she said. "It's empty. I'd invite you to stay there instead of the hotel, but you might have some company again."

"I explained that to you."

"I know you did," she said. "I was teasing you. Still, it wouldn't be a bad idea. We could watch each other's back better."

Clint pointed with his fork and said, "You know, that wouldn't be a bad idea. Louis Cameron would suddenly have no idea where I was."

"Might make him nervous," she said. "You'd have your own room, and I promise not to try to crawl into bed with you."

"I'll take you at your word."

"Besides, you might not have any energy left after . . ."

"I told you—"

But she was laughing too hard to listen to him.

At dinner that night in the Cameron house Louis looked across the table at his wife, Olivia, and said, "I understand you were at the Plaza today."

"That's right, I was."

"With Clint Adams?"

"Yes," she said. "Is that a problem?"

"Not if you tell me everything the two of you talked about," he said.

"That's no problem at all, dear," she said. "In fact, that's the very reason I went to his room with him."

"I'm sure."

"He told me he's sure that you, or someone in this family, killed that Archer woman."

"Is that right?" Cameron asked.

"What did he say to you today, dear?"

"Much the same thing," the old man said.

"What are you going to do?" she asked. "You're not going to . . . damage him, are you?"

"I'm afraid you're going to have to find yourself a new lover, dear," Cameron said. "I'm going to do much more than just damage him."

"That's a shame," she said, "but you're certainly not going to do it yourself, are you?"

"I wish I could," Cameron said, "but no, I have the perfect person in mind for the job."

"Who would that be, dear?"

"Never mind," Cameron said. "Just eat your dinner. This conversation is over."

"Of course it is, dear."

• • •

Olivia's mind was racing. She had hoped to pry loose from her husband the name of the man her husband had hired to kill Clint Adams. He gave her nothing, though, except for the fact that he was, in fact, going to do it. She was going to have to figure out a way to get out of the house after dinner to go and warn Clint.

She could not let anything happen to that magical, wonderful man now that she'd found him.

At least, not until she went to bed with him one more time.

Clint and Sandy were in his room, gathering up his belongings. Clint realized during dessert that he could not simply check out of the hotel. The clerk would certainly tip off Louis Cameron about his departure.

"So let's just sneak you out the back door," Sandy suggested.

First they made sure there was a back door, then they made sure it wasn't locked. They decided to go in the back door and collect his things, before going back out that way.

"Saddlebags and rifle," Sandy observed. "You travel light."

"The only things I own that I can't do without are my gun and my horse," Clint said. "And logically speaking, I could get another horse—although I wouldn't want to have to try to get one as good."

"You've been lucky with horses," Sandy said. "First Duke, then Eclipse."

"No luck," Clint said. "I raised Duke. Okay, maybe getting Eclipse as a gift could be called luck."

"Are you ready?"

"Let's go."

They took the back stairs down and went out. Then they took an alley to a side street and from there they caught a horse-drawn cab to the house. Clint's secret escape from the hotel was complete.

THIRTY-SIX

True to her word, Sandy did not try to crawl into bed with Clint—and the same went with him. They had too much respect for their dead friend.

Clint woke feeling sad. He was in Anne's house. He could almost feel her presence. And when this was all over, what was he supposed to do with a fifteen-year-old daughter?

He could smell the coffee, so he dressed and went into the kitchen to join Sandy at the table.

"Did you sleep?" she asked.

"Some."

"I don't like it when this house is empty," she said.

"What are you going to do with it when this is all over?" he asked.

"What am I gonna do with it?" she asked. "It's not mine."

"Whose is it?"

"Well, I guess it belongs to Little Sandy now," Sandy said. "But you're her father. I think it's gonna be up to you."

"Me?"

"What are you gonna do with this house?" she asked. "And what are you gonna do with your daughter?"

"What can I do with a fifteen-year-old girl?" he asked.

"Almost sixteen."

"I was hoping you and Katy would take her."

"We'd love to," she said, "either one of us, but you know what the life of a Pinkerton is like. Where could she live? Neither Katy or I have a home anywhere."

Clint played with his coffee mug.

"Jesus," he said, "I never thought I'd end up being responsible for a teenage girl."

"Well, maybe you better get used to it."

He drank some coffee, slammed the mug down.

"First I have to find out who killed Anne, make sure they pay and come out alive myself. I'll have to think about the house and Sandy later."

"Well, I can't fault you for that," she said. "If you get killed, Katy and I won't have a choice, we'll have to take over."

"I appreciate the sentiment," he said.

"You know what I mean," she said. "Of course I don't want you to get killed because you're a wonderful human bein—"

"Okay, I get it."

"He's gonna do it, you know," she said.

"Do what?"

"Send somebody for you. Somebody who thinks he can take you, not like that kid Bravo."

"I know it."

"Why didn't you kill that kid, anyway?"

"Because I didn't have to."

"It might have sent a message to Cameron."

"Like what? I kill children?"

"Well, it won't be a child next time," she said. "What if this time it is someone faster than you?"

He shrugged.

"It's bound to happen sometime."

"Well, I wouldn't like it to be now," she said.

"If he sends a killer for me this time—I mean, somebody who really knows how to use a gun—then I think he's sending us a definite message."

"Which is, he wants you dead?"

"Which is," Clint said, "either he had Anne killed, or he's covering for somebody in his family who did."

"Like his wife?"

"I don't think he cares enough for her."

"Okay, then his son's wife," Sandy said. "She has a definite motive."

"I don't think she cares enough."

"Then . . . you're talking about Billy? He was in love with Anne."

"But she wasn't in love with him, right?"

"Right."

"So what if he found out?"

"But . . . he's drinking himself into a stupor because she's dead."

"What if he's drinking himself into a stupor because he killed her?"

She sat back in her chair.

"I never considered that," she said. "Well then, we really do need to talk to him."

"We can try this morning," Clint said, "hopefully before he has time to crawl into another bottle."

"We'd better get a move on if we want to do that," she said.

They stood up, each grabbing the gun they'd hung on a chair and strapping it on.

"Oh, and one thing," she said.

"Yeah?"

"If his wife tries to stop us again, let me handle her."

THIRTY-SEVEN

Denver Cole walked into Louis Cameron's office, didn't say a word and sat down opposite the big desk. He knew he was there to make money, and the old man would tell him when and how, so he had no questions.

"You know who Clint Adams is?" Cameron asked.

"Everybody knows who he is," Cole said, "especially men in my business."

"Well, he's become a thorn in my side," the old man said. "I want him dead."

"Man like that's gonna cost extra."

"Name your price."

"When do you want this done?"

"Today."

Cole thought a moment.

"Blank check," he said.

"That's high."

"You don't have to give it to me until after I kill him."

Cameron sat back in his chair.

"That's fair."

Cole leaned forward.

"We're always fair with each other, Mr. Cameron," he said. "That's why we get along."

Cameron was actually surprised that they got along at all. They were, after all, two men who ruled their worlds by fear, and they had each found someone who didn't fear them.

"Where do I find him?" Cole asked.

"He checked into my Plaza hotel, but I don't know if he's still there."

"Where's he been drinkin'?"

"The Red Garter."

"Your saloon?"

Cameron nodded.

"This fella's really in your face."

"And I want him out of it."

Cole nodded and headed for the door.

"Cole."

The gunman turned.

"I don't much care how it gets done."

"It don't do me any good to do it any way but head-on," Cole said.

"Don't forget your fee is a blank check," Cameron said. "Why take chances?"

"Money's just money, Mr. Cameron," Cole said. "This is the Gunsmith we're talkin' about. He don't deserve nothin' but head-on."

"Even you?" Cameron said. "What does this man have that rates respect from the likes of you?"

Cole turned back to face Cameron, his posture suddenly aggressive.

"What is the likes of me, Cameron," he asked, "except for someone you hire to do your dirty work?"

"I meant no disrespect, man," Cameron said, waving

away the man's aggression. "Clint Adams frustrates me. He came here to my office, he tried to get to me through my wife . . ."

Cole knew how that must've worked. He wouldn't have minded trying to get to the old man that way himself.

". . . and then he went to my son's house and upset my daughter-in-law."

The daughter-in-law, Cole thought, *there was another one*. He didn't know how these Cameron men rated wives that young and beautiful. Yes, he did. *It was the money.*

"Well, I'll get this job done," he told the old man, "but I'll get it done my way."

"However you get it done," Cameron said, "just do it today."

"It'll get done today," Cole said. "You just have that check ready."

"It'll be waiting."

Cole nodded, opened the door and went out. Walters, unlike Cameron, had nothing but fear when it came to Denver Cole, as he seemed to shrink when the gunman walked by. Once Cole was gone, Walters got up and went into the old man's office.

"Get me a check," Cameron said.

"Who shall I make it out to," Walters asked, "and for how much?"

"Make it out to Cole, but leave the amount blank."

"You'll fill it in?"

"He will."

Walter's eyebrows shot up.

"A blank check?"

"Do you want the job, Walters?" Cameron asked. "How much would you charge?"

Backing out of the room, Walters said, "I'll get that check ready, sir."

As he closed the door to his master's office, the other door opened and Olivia Cameron walked in.

"Olivia," he hissed, "my God, it's been ages! When can we—"

"I'm afraid we can't, Franklin."

"What?"

"It's over," she said. "I can't be with you, anymore. Do you know if Clint Adams is still at the Plaza?"

"I, uh, we can't—"

"Pay attention, Franklin," she said. "I tried to find Mr. Adams at his hotel last night and this morning and he wasn't there. Do you know where he is?"

"Uh, no, no, I don't," Walters said.

She frowned, then turned to leave. He grabbed her elbow, and she pulled away from him.

"But Olivia, I thought we—"

"We're over, Franklin," she said.

"Is there . . . someone else?"

"I have a husband, Franklin," she reminded him, "and if you persist in bothering me, I will tell him. Do you want to lose your job, or worse?"

"No," he said, "no, I just . . . don't understand."

"What's there to understand, dear?" she asked, touching his face. "It was fun, and it's over." She slapped him, not hard, but forcefully. "Get that through your head."

She turned and walked out, leaving him totally confused.

THIRTY-EIGHT

After breakfast Clint and Sandy got their horses and rode to Billy Cameron's house, which was on the other side of the city. When they knocked, the same black woman answered the door.

"Mr. Billy's not here," she said.

"Do you know where he went?" Clint asked.

The woman turned and looked over her shoulder, then dropped her voice down to a conspiratorial whisper.

"If you ask me, he's already got one of them saloons ta open their doors fer him."

"We're too late," Sandy said.

"Too late?" the maid asked.

"We wanted to talk to him while he was sober."

"Mister," she said, "you way too late for that. Mr. Billy, he wakes up drunk these days."

"Okay," Clint said. "Thanks."

"Can you tell us which saloon he might be in?"

"Can't tell you that," she said, "but I can tell you the grubbier the better."

• • •

Olivia was walking the streets in a frenzy, looking for
Clint Adams. She'd never done this for a man before.
Usually, they were chasing her. But it worked, because
she saw him riding down the street on his horse—with a
woman by his side. A big, coarse-looking blonde. Was
that why she couldn't find him last night? Because he was
with this woman?

Well, she'd be damned if she'd chase him down the
street now to warn him about her husband. Let him take
his chances on his own.

She turned and headed back to her husband's office.
Maybe she could catch Franklin Walters before what she
said to him really sunk in.

Clint and Sandy reined in their horses in front of the
Plaza hotel. With Billy Cameron hiding out in a fleabag
saloon somewhere in the city, Clint was going back to his
old plan. He'd let Louis Cameron know exactly where he
was and wait for the hired gun who was sure to come after him.

When they entered the lobby, the clerk didn't blink
at them. He had no idea that Clint had sneaked out the
back door the night before. As far as anyone was concerned, Clint had been in his hotel suite all night.

That went for Lieutenant Abernathy as well, who was
sitting there in the lobby.

"Lieutenant Abernathy," Clint said as the man fronted
him. "This is Sandy Spillane."

"Ma'am," the man said. He looked at Clint. "I've been
looking for you all morning."

"Why?"

"To warn you," the policeman said. "We've got word that Denver Cole rode into town today."

"Don't know him."

"He's a gunman," Sandy said. "For hire."

"And he only comes to a town when he's hired," Abernathy said.

"So we're figuring this is Louis Cameron's big gun?" Clint asked.

"If he paid Cole to kill you, and we can prove it, I can move on Cameron."

"You want to arrest him for the murder of Annie?" Sandy asked.

"Sandy and Anne Archer were partners, Lieutenant."

"Partners?"

"Sandy is a Pinkerton, too."

The man looked miffed.

"Pinkertons operating in Kansas City without notifying us? The chief's not going to like that."

"That's beside the point right now," Sandy said. "You have enough to arrest Cameron?"

"I do," Abernathy said, "but not the Cameron you're thinking of."

"Billy?" Clint asked.

"Yes."

"That's why he's been drunk since the murder," Clint said. "Because he did it."

"That's what I believe," Abernathy said. "And I think if I can get him away from his father, he'll crack."

"So if it looks like his father's trying to cover for him by having me killed . . ."

"I'll bring them both in."

"Your chief goes along with this?"

"He does."

"So I have to make sure his hired killer doesn't kill me," Clint said, "while trying not to kill him."

"You did it with Joe Bravo," Sandy said, "but—"

"—but Denver Cole," Abernathy finished, "is not Joe Bravo."

THIRTY-NINE

After Abernathy left, Sandy said, "You'd think he'd offer to help, since we're doing his job for him."

"He didn't have to come and warn me," Clint said. "What do you know about Denver Cole?"

"He's deadly," she said. "He doesn't know how many men he's killed because he doesn't count 'em."

"And how does he kill them?"

"Head-on, as far as I know," she said. "I've never heard anything about him bushwhacking anybody."

"Well, maybe I won't have to worry about that, then," he said.

"Don't worry, I'll watch your back. Hell, I'll stand in the street with you."

"I won't need you to do that," Clint said, "not if Cole is the man you say he his."

"I'm only tellin' you what we heard at the Pinkerton's," she told him.

"And that's all I can go by."

"He's young and he's fast, Clint," she said. "How the hell are you supposed to keep him from killin' you and not kill him?"

"I don't know," he said. "I guess I'll have to think of a way."

Denver Cole could not let it show in Louis Cameron's office, but he was excited. He'd killed many men—didn't know how many because he didn't count them. Some of them had been fast, some had been deadly accurate, but none of them had the reputation of the Gunsmith. He was supposed to be both fast and accurate.

Cole had ridden into town that morning and hadn't bothered to get himself a room. In the past he did all his jobs the same day he arrived, so there was no waiting—not for him and not for the intended victim. And there was no spending of his money for a room or a bed he wasn't going to use.

He was sure Clint Adams knew that someone was coming for him, but maybe he didn't know who it was. And even if he had heard who was coming, he'd probably never heard of Cole. That was fine with the gunman. After today everybody was going to know his name and what he did.

Denver Cole, the man who killed the Gunsmith.

FORTY

"You're just gonna sit there?" Sandy asked.

Clint had found a wooden chair and carried it out to the front of the Red Garter. He put it down in front of the building, with a wall against his back, not a window, and sat.

"Cameron's gun has to be able to find me," Clint explained, "or nothing is going to happen."

"What am I supposed to do?"

"You get a chair and sit over there," he said, pointing across the street. "Whatever happens, you make sure nobody shoots me in the back from a window."

"I thought you said you didn't believe Cole would do that?"

"I don't think *he* would," Clint said, "but Cameron might put somebody up in a window with a rifle, just in case."

Unable to help herself, Sandy suddenly looked up.

"Yeah," he said, "see if you can find windows with a good angle."

"How will I know where you're gonna stand?"

"I'll try to stand there," he said, pointing, "if we end

up in the street. If he's smart, he'll try to maneuver me to where he wants me. You're just going to have to watch and figure."

Sandy dried her palms on her thighs.

"Don't be nervous," he said. "I trust you."

"Yeah," she said. "I'm used to working in a trio, you know? Me, Annie and Katy. Unbeatable."

"Don't worry," he said again, "you were each always unbeatable on your own."

"Yeah," she said, "look where that got Annie. Katy and I left her alone, and—"

"You can't blame yourself for that," he said. "Nobody can defend against a bullet in the back. Even with you watching mine, there could still be a good marksman on a roof three hundred yards from here who could put one dead-center."

"Jesus . . ." she said, shaking her head. "I'm used to tracking people, you know? This shoot-out in the street business . . . not for me."

"Well, then," he said, "let's make this your last, and let's make your last the best."

Denver Cole was having a drink a few blocks away from the Red Garter. He found a small saloon that was doing little business that early and stood at the bar nursing a small whiskey. He didn't want to drink too much, because he was going to have to be sharp for Clint Adams. One whiskey always sharpened him up, but he never knocked it back, he always savored it—just like he would savor every moment against Clint Adams.

In the beginning he'd maneuver him to where he wanted him. Next would be the moment just before he drew his gun. That's when everything would go quiet, everybody would just fade away and all he'd be able to see was Clint Adams, standing there waiting for his last bullet.

And then the moment just after, when he saw that puff of dust kicked up by the bullet as it entered Adams's chest and put him down for the last time.

Finally, he'd walk to the fallen Gunsmith, stand over him and let everyone take a good, hard, long look. That would be a pose worthy of a painting. Too bad he didn't have time to alert an artist, or even a photographer. Wouldn't that make a great picture for the front page of dozens of newspapers across the county!

Louis Cameron handed the man five hundred dollars.

"Pick a window where you can see the Red Garter and the street in front."

"What if they don't do it there?" the man asked.

"Don't worry," Cameron said, "Denver Cole will want as large an audience as he can get."

"So if Adams kills Cole, I kill Adams," the man said.

"And you get another five hundred."

The man nodded, stuffed the five hundred dollars into his shirt pocket, picked up his rifle, turned and started for the door. When he got there, he turned around.

"What if Cole wins?"

Cameron thought about the blank check Cole wanted to hold him up for.

"If he wins," Cameron said, "wait until he walks to the body and stands over it, then kill him."

"What if he don't stand over him?"

"Oh, don't worry about that either," Cameron said. "If he kills the Gunsmith, he's going to want to stand over him for the entire town to see. You just put a bullet in him

when he does. Then come back here for your other five
hundred."

"Okay," the man said.

As the man with the rifle left, Cameron opened his
drawer and stared at the gun there. Maybe to complete
the circle he'd just put a bullet in the rifleman when he
came back for his second five hundred, then take the first
five hundred back. Leave it to Walters to dispose of the
body. He was good at little errands like that.

Sandy walked across the street, found a chair that was already sitting against the window of the Plaza hotel.
Seemed a fitting place to watch the action. She scanned the
windows and rooftops across the street, which all looked
clear to her, but from where she sat she'd never be able to
see above her, or anywhere on her side of the street. She
suddenly realized that Clint had sent her over here to keep
her out of the way. Okay, then, she'd show him she had
value and possessed initiative. If she was a man with a rifle
whose job it was to put a bullet in Clint Adams's back
while he stood in the street, where would she be?

She got up from her chair, went inside and asked the
clerk, "How do I get to the roof?"

FORTY-ONE

Clint spotted Denver Cole walking down the street. It could only be him. It was in his walk, his posture, hell, it was written all over his face.

Whether or not he could keep Cole alive and keep himself alive at the same time depended on how good Cole really was.

Clint remained in his chair, relaxed. He doubted he could talk the man out of what he had in mind. The price was bound to be too high.

He loosened his gun in his holster and waited . . .

Denver Cole saw Clint Adams sitting in a chair in front of the hotel. It had to be him, waiting. That was fine. It suited him not to have to go looking for the man. He knew earning his money wouldn't be easy, but at least it would be quick.

The man with the rifle stood on the roof and sighted down the barrel. At the moment he was aiming at Denver Cole, because that was the only man he could see. Soon, however, Cole would entice Adams out into the

street and he'd have both possible targets in front of
him.

It would be up to the two men who would actually become the target. The rifleman made a bet with himself
that he would end up being the man who killed the Gunsmith, not Denver Cole.

Sandy got to the top floor of the hotel and started looking
for the hatch in the ceiling that would take her to the roof.
When she found it, she had a problem. She couldn't reach
it. She jumped a few times, but she was too short. She
looked around but there were no chairs in the hallway.
This had to be a problem for most people who had to get
to the roof. There had to be a ladder somewhere, maybe
in a closet.

She started trying doors.

There was a tension between the two men, who were still
a distance from each other, that people on the
street could sense. Slowly, the spectators started to go inside. It didn't matter where, they just needed to get
inside. Strangers opened their doors to strangers, until the street was virtually empty, except for the two men.

Clint watched as Denver Cole approached. Once Cole got
there, Clint let the two front legs of his chair hit the
boardwalk.

Cole stopped in the street, right in front of Clint.

"Clint Adams?"

"That's right," Clint said. "You Cole?"

"I'm Cole."

"How much is Cameron paying you?"

"Blank check."

"Impressive," Clint said, "but still not enough to die for."

Cole shrugged and said, "This is how I make a living."

"Dying ain't much of a living."

"Well," Cole said, "this time it's about much more than that."

"Oh, you want a reputation?" Clint asked. "The man who killed Clint Adams?"

"The man who killed the Gunsmith," Cole corrected.

"You think you're going to see that on a dime novel in a few months?"

Cole shrugged.

"All I know is everybody in this country will know my name next week," Cole said, "and I'll be a rich man. I don't see any bad side to this."

"I do."

"What?"

"You'll be dead in a few minutes."

Cole pushed his hat back on his head, rubbed his jaw and regarded Clint critically.

"I don't know," he said, "I got about fifteen years on you. You can't be as good as you used to be."

"You got it wrong, junior," Clint said. "I'm the one who's got fifteen years on you—in experience."

"Yeah," Cole said, "but are you as fast as you used to be?"

"I don't have to be faster than you," Clint said, "just more accurate."

"You think I'm gonna miss?"

"I think we're talking this thing to death," Clint said. "But before we do this, I just need you to say it again, for the record."

"Say what?"

"That Louis Cameron hired you to kill me."

"Why not?" Cole asked. "Why should I deny a dying man's last wish? Cameron hired me to kill you."

"The old man? Louis. Not the son?"

"The son's useless," Cole said. "It was the old man. He said you're a thorn in his side."

"He's right." Clint stood up. "Okay, where do you want me? In the street?"

"That's as good a place as any."

"Can I give you a piece of advice before we start?" Clint asked.

"Sure."

"If you do get lucky and manage to kill me," he said, "watch the rooftops."

"The rooft—you sayin' you put a man on the roof with a rifle?"

"Not me," Clint said.

"Cameron?"

"You really think he's going to give you a blank check?" Clint asked. "Come on, you know him better than I do."

"That can't be!"

"Can't it?" Clint asked. "I'll bet you your blank check that whether I kill you or you kill me, the winner will be dead seconds later."

Cole frowned.

"If that's true, there won't be nobody alive to collect on that bet," he said.

"Won't there?"

FORTY-TWO

Sandy was frantic. She had to get to the roof and she still wasn't finding a chair or a ladder. She felt stupid. She ran down to the lobby where there were plenty of chairs.

"Hey!" the clerk shouted as she grabbed one and ran up the stairs with it.

Clint stepped down into the street, moved off to his right, while Denver Cole backed up and moved left. Some brave people came outside to watch from a closer vantage point, but for the most part the street was empty.

Clint and Cole stopped, facing each other over a distance of not less than twenty feet.

The man on the roof with the rifle sighted down the barrel. *Come on*, he thought, *somebody make a move and give me my target.*

Sandy set the chair beneath the hatch and climbed up on it. She reached up to push the hatch open, but it was either heavy or stuck.

Damn it, she thought, *either way I'm getting this hatch open!*

The onlookers watched and waited to see who was going to make the first move. Some bets were made, but for the most part this was just a little piece of history people were watching—especially if the Gunsmith got himself killed!

Suddenly, Cole's hand streaked for his gun.

The man with the rifle watched as Denver Cole cleanly outdrew the Gunsmith and shot him down. As Adams hit the street on his back, Cole marched to where Adams lay and stood over the Gunsmith, just like Cameron predicted he would.

Just turn a little bit, he thought, *give me your back.*

"Hold it!" the rifleman heard from behind him.

He turned quickly and pulled the trigger, but Sandy was down on one knee. The hatch had been heavy, which helped her. If it had been light, she would have flipped it over and made a lot of noise doing it. As it was, she'd had to lift and slide the heavy lid off and hadn't made a sound.

The rifleman's shot went over her head. As he levered another round, she fired once. The bullet struck him in the chest. He staggered back and fell off the roof.

Denver Cole looked up at the sound of the shot, saw a man and a rifle fall from the roof of the Plaza hotel.

"You were right," he said to Clint.

On the ground Clint opened his eyes, looked up at Cole and said, "You owe me your blank check."

To the surprise of all and the consternation of some, Cole reached down and helped Clint to his feet.

"Good luck collectin'," Cole said. "If Cameron was willin' to kill me to save it, he ain't gonna let go of it real easy."

"That's okay," Clint said. "I didn't really want it, anyway. All I want you to do is tell the police he hired you to kill me."

"I don't have to admit to anythin' else?"

"No, we'll tell them you came right to me and told me, and we set up this little bit of playacting."

"And you had somebody on the roof all along?"

"I had somebody watching my back," Clint said. "How she got to the roof I don't know, but I'm sure glad she did."

Cole hesitated a moment, then said, "She?"

FORTY-THREE

Clint followed Lieutenant Abernathy into Louis Cameron's office with Franklin Walters trailing along behind them saying, "B-but you can't—"

Clint stopped just inside the room, turned, pushed Walters back outside and slammed the door in his face.

"He's got a gun in a drawer of that desk," Clint said, "but I don't think he has the nerve to use it."

"What's the meaning of this?" Cameron demanded with all the indignation he could muster.

"You're under arrest, Mr. Cameron," Abernathy said.

"On what charge?"

"Conspiracy to commit murder."

Cameron stared at Clint. He obviously assumed that Denver Cole was dead.

"Your man gave you up."

"My man?" He wondered if they'd grabbed the man with the rifle.

"Denver Cole." Abernathy clarified things. "He told us everything."

"The man's a notorious gunman and liar," Cameron said.

"How about your son?" Abernathy asked. "Is he a liar, too?"

"He's a drunk," Cameron said.

"Yeah, yeah," Abernathy said, "everybody's either a liar or a drunk and you're a victim. Get up, Cameron."

"You can't do this," Cameron said, starting to get nervous. "I know people."

"Yeah, I know people, too," the lieutenant said, "lots of people."

"My lawyer will—"

"We'll arrange a meeting between you and your lawyer . . . in your cell."

Abernathy came around the desk, stopped to look out the window.

"Oh, look," he said, "one of my men has Billy. Maybe we can put you in the same cell."

Abernathy had sent uniformed policemen all over the city to search low-rent saloons for Billy Cameron.

The old man stood up with a speed that belied his age and looked out the window. He saw Billy Cameron talking to a uniformed policeman, who had him in handcuffs.

"Goddamnit!" he said.

"Let's go," Abernathy said, taking out his cuffs. "I got a nice pair of bracelets for you, too."

"No," the old mans said. "No." He turned and lunged for his desk drawer. Clint was there first, swatting his hand away before removing the gun from the drawer.

"Jesus," he said, looking at the old Colt Navy, "this would've blown up in your hand, old man."

"I can give you the killer," Cameron said. "I can tell you who killed that woman, but you have to let me—"

"We don't have to let you do nothin'," Abernathy said.

"It was Billy!" the old man shouted. "My son, Billy. He got drunk, the girl rejected him. It was him!"

Abernathy looked at Clint and raised his eyebrows.

"You were right," Abernathy said to Clint.

"Right?" Cameron asked. "About what?"

"He said you'd give up your own flesh and blood to try to stay out of jail," Abernathy said. "That don't exactly make you father of the year in my book."

He grabbed the old man's hands and slapped the handcuffs on him.

"No, no," Cameron said. "My son is young, he can take prison. I can't."

"Don't worry," Clint said, "you'll be able to help each other. And I want you to think about Anne Archer while you're in there. She was worth ten of your son and a million of you."

"That's what this is about?" the old man demanded. "That woman?"

"That woman was a friend of mine," Clint said, "a close friend of mine. You and your boy made a big mistake, Cameron, and you're both going to pay."

"B-but—I have money . . ."

"Yeah," Abernathy said, "tell it to the judge. It might mean something to him."

As Abernathy marched Cameron out, Clint realized the man was right. Cameron's money might mean something to a politician or a judge.

That was something to worry about.

Later that week Clint was still worrying about that.

"So if he buys his way out, then what?" Sandy asked.

"Then I'll have to come back and make sure justice is served the old way," Clint said.

"You'd do that?" she asked. "Kill them?"

"Both of them."

They were outside the house that Anne Archer had shared with her daughter, Sandy. Clint's horse was saddled and ready to go.

Katy came out of the house with Little Sandy, whose head was hanging down. Clint had stayed up most of the night with his daughter, explaining why he couldn't take her with him, why she'd be better off with Katy and Sandy in Chicago, where they were based for Pinkerton. The two aunts had agreed that one of them would always be available for the girl, who would soon be a young woman anyway.

"Say good-bye to your father, Sandy," Katy said.

"Good-bye," she said sullenly.

"Sandy—" Katy said, but Clint waved her off.

"Sandy, I know you don't believe me but I do love you. I'll come to see you often."

She looked up at him.

"Do you promise?"

"I swear it," he said. "Are you going to let me ride out without a hug?"

For a moment, he thought she would, but then she suddenly lunged forward and hugged him, then pulled his head down so she could kiss him soundly on the cheek.

" 'Bye, Poppa."

The night before she had settled on "Poppa" for what she would call him.

"I'll see you soon, sweetie," he said, hugging her tight.

He stepped to his horse and mounted up.

"I'll see you all soon," he said.

"You'd better," Katy said, "or we'll come lookin' for you."

He waved, turned his horse and rode away from his daughter with an aching heart.

Watch for

STRAW MEN

320th novel in the exciting GUNSMITH series
from Jove

Coming in August!

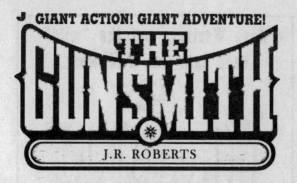

GIANT ACTION! GIANT ADVENTURE!

THE GUNSMITH

J.R. ROBERTS

Little Sureshot And
The Wild West Show
(Gunsmith Giant #9)

Dead Weight
(Gunsmith Giant #10)

Red Mountain
(Gunsmith Giant #11)

The Knights of Misery
(Gunsmith Giant #12)

penguin.com

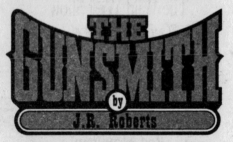

Penguin Group (USA) Online

What will you be reading tomorrow?

Tom Clancy, Patricia Cornwell, W.E.B. Griffin,
Nora Roberts, William Gibson, Robin Cook,
Brian Jacques, Catherine Coulter, Stephen King,
Dean Koontz, Ken Follett, Clive Cussler,
Eric Jerome Dickey, John Sandford,
Terry McMillan, Sue Monk Kidd, Amy Tan,
John Berendt…

You'll find them all at
penguin.com

Read excerpts and newsletters,
find tour schedules and reading group guides,
and enter contests.

Subscribe to Penguin Group (USA) newsletters
and get an exclusive inside look
at exciting new titles and the authors you love
long before everyone else does.

PENGUIN GROUP (USA)
us.penguingroup.com

M224G1107